FATHER MAY BE AN ELEPHANT AND MOTHER ONLY A SMALL BASKET, BUT...

Enugantha Tandri Kanna
Ekula Buttanta Talli Nayam

GW00655900

(Interior Title Page)

CONTENTS

1. Father May Be an Elephant and Mother Only a Small Basket, But… … 7
   Enugantha Tandri Kanna Ekula Buttanta Talli Nayam
2. Trace it! … 19
   Jaada
3. Braveheart Badeyya … 29
   Madiga Badeyya
5. Jambava's Lineage … 53
   Jambava Munum
6. Tataki Wins Again … 67
   Tataki
7. The Village Tank's Lament … 79
   Oorajeruvu Kadupu Kota
8. Obstacle Race … 87
   Gandalu
9. Raw Wound … 103
   Radam
10. Ellamma is Distressed … 127
    Ellamma Daskindi
11. The Bottom of the Well … 139
    Bayi Talam
12. A Beauteous Light … 147
    Deepa Sundari
13. Gogu Shyamala's World … 187
14. A Note on the Translation … 201
15. Lines that Cut to the Very Gut: K. Lalita … 203
16. The Translators … 209
17. Acknowledgements … 213

FATHER MAY BE AN ELEPHANT AND MOTHER ONLY A SMALL BASKET, BUT...

Enugantha Tandri Kanna
Ekula Buttanta Talli Nayam

All the children gathered on the bunds outside the village as soon as the sun broke briefly through the clouds. It was just before dusk. There had been no rains for a long time. The droplets on the grass glistened in the light. The clouds in motion, now hiding, now revealing, the sun. The boys played chedugudu in one corner and the girls hide-and-seek, running to catch each other. The younger boys always played with the girls, and today it was Baindla Ramulu's turn to catch us. We hid behind the bushes, between large sleepy rocks and under the mountain-high bunds. Lost in our game, nothing in the world could distract us. We had not played like this for many a rainy day, and we were desperate not to let even a moment go to waste. The newly washed sun pierced once again through the dark clouds. A rainbow blossomed: it was perfect! We counted from one side and from the other, trying to find all the seven colours. Despite many tries, Potbelly Narsi could only find six. When I found all seven, I began jumping with joy until I heard someone singing one of Pandugala Sayanna's songs somewhere in the distance. It was Talari Anthanna on the bund of the village tank. He was mounted on his buffalo, a long vayili stick in his hand, and singing a kinnera.

I strained to listen. It was my favourite song, this one. When my ears picked up the words I sang along.

Orori Sayanna, oh Panduga Sayanna!
Paalamuri eedigas'
carts of rice are going,
twelve puttis of rice are going,
going to Tandur!
Don't let go: even if you lose your life
Don't let go Sayanna,
Kin kin kin…

Ponnalolla Balamani always competed with me. When we played; when we sang; when we ran. Now, as we were running about and playing, we sang together:

Kottapeta market,
on your head a blanket.
Sayalu, you run,
I run, Sayalu.

Children flitted around the bunds like dragonflies. The grass under their feet bounced up and down after them. The droplets had disappeared in the sun. We played and played till it was time for our mothers to return from the fields. We stood on the bunds trying to pick out the women walking towards us from a distance. As if a thousand crows had flocked to the clouds, the sky suddenly darkened. Near the mala–madiga drinking-water well the road split into two. The mala women went towards the mala keri and the madiga women towards the madiga keri. My mother was not among them. I stood there waiting. The rain was heavy but the women did not change their pace. They were drenched anyway. As was I, my body cold and tired, but I just stood there, waiting. Darkness surrounded us as the rain lashed down. But I didn't notice any of this as I waited for my mother. The women had been weeding the paddy fields all day, taking on the entire day's rainfall. They squeezed out their wet kulla and placed them back over their heads. As though furrowing their way back home, they walked briskly, one behind the other, along the narrow ridges of the paddy fields. I was still looking for my mother. All the women had their heads covered with kulla and they all looked the same to me. My mother had stitched a new green kulla. She had also torn up an old sari and made a new kunchi. Although my eyes were looking for Mother, my thoughts wandered to that kunchi. First, she had cut the soft bits of the torn sari into neat rectangles; to those she attached the stronger bits and lined both with a piece of my father's old white dhoti. Then she attached the silk border of the sari to the top of the kunchi and stitched it all together. It looked beautiful from behind when she wrapped it around her head. The silk border shined brightly as it hung down our backs. I draped my head with it and pretended I was a princess. My elder sister always fought with me for it. We would snatch it away from each other to cover ourselves at night. Unable to pacify us, my mother stitched two small kulla for both of us. My mother is brilliant at stitching kunchi. Our neighbour Ningampalli Sayavva praised her often, "Her fingers spin like tops … she is the fastest at stitching kunchis."

By now I had watched the entire village return from work. But my mother did not come. Then at a distance I saw a woman walking alone, like a whirlwind in the darkness. I knew it had to be her. She was not at all pleased to see me all drenched. I rushed to her and clung to her waist. "Why are you here, my dear? You should have lit the lamp at home and waited with your little brother. Stubborn girl, clinging to me

like the rain. What did you think I would bring from the forest
—food?" I wanted to search her kulla. But Mother held on to
my arm and dragged me home. My younger brother was sitting
on the threshold, worried and weeping. The boy was a coward.
He was even scared of thunder and lightning. When my
mother saw him like that she scolded me even more. She let go
of my hand and quickly picked him up.

"Are you scared, son?" she said stroking his back. She
turned to me. "Look at this fellow, how scared he is. And what
are you doing just standing there? Have you lost something—
look at you—you look like an owl drenched in the rain." Her
scolding me made my brother so happy, he forgot his fear. He
said, "Amma, I am hungry," and I was reminded of my own
hunger. My anger disappeared. Quickly she put him down, took
out some tender green gram from her kunchi and gave it to us.
She kept some aside for our elder brother. Only after we had
eaten our fill did she notice the smell of wet earth in the house.

Our house always smelt like that when it rained. Damp had
seeped deep into the house—up to the nooks where we stored
stuff, where we cooked, and by the low dividing wall. Small
puddles dotted the floor of the house. Black, grease-like dirt
blotched the walls. Mother placed german silver vessels and
earthen pots at the spots where rain was dripping from the
roof. I joined in, looking for things to place under the
remaining spots. The house was filled with the music of rain
falling into the many pots and vessels. *Tapa tapa tan tan tin tin…*
Mother moved through the music throwing out the water that
had collected in her pots and vessels. I was eating tender green
gram with one hand and chucking out water with the other.

"Look, behind the ventilator, it's leaking there," my younger
brother called out. Mother ran to put a metal container under

the ventilator. "The house has become a sieve. Where should I put what? Every year he used to re-thatch the hut. But he is not here this year, and look at the mess this house has become," Mother grumbled as she walked around. The rain did not subside. Amidst the sounds of rain and thunder outside, and the sound of dripping water inside, we could barely hear each other.

"The boy must be drenched by now... Has he reached the village? Is he still in the forest? I have no idea ... and the old woman has not come back either." Just as Mother was saying this, Sangavva entered. She had gone in search of work but had not found any. She had been to the dorasani's house, cleaned out the sand from three sacks of jowar and for that she got some of yesterday's rotte and a small vessel of watery dal. She brought it home wrapped within the pleats of her sari. From the kulla bundle she took out a few fistfuls of paddy and poured it into the winnowing basket. Mother gathered it all into the grain pot, covered the pot, and put it in a dry corner. Just then, our elder brother came home, completely drenched. My mother called out loudly, "Ramchandrappa is home!"

"Hang that wet gunny bag on the wall, wash your feet with the water in the pot and come in, son," she said. Sangavva asked, "Was the rotte that you took enough for you, child?" My brother sounded irritated, "Where avva? Did the calves allow me to sit and eat? They kept trying to push their way into the patel's fields. I let them graze along the bunds. At three in the afternoon I took them to the pond to drink water. When they finally lay down under the trees to chew cud, I opened my rotte bundle. Just then the rain stole down on me like a thief. I quickly packed up the rotte and came back towards the village."

Drying my brother's head with a towel, mother said angrily, "Those rascal calves don't stay where they should. They have killed my son's hunger, haven't they? My son is stunted, roaming like this from place to place. Once this year is over, we can get rid of this trouble. Next year your father will be back from the big city. He'll pay off our debts. Not too many days now; the harvest is over. The next new moon, it will be one year since he left." Mother consoled him, stroking his back.

My mother did not believe a single word she was saying. It was all for my brother's sake. Sangavva lit the stove and we all sat around it for warmth. Brother gave us younger ones some of the rotte he had brought back, and ate the rest. We also took a share of his green gram. After a while he asked, "Mother, when will Father come back from town? Why have Venkatreddy Patel's people stopped harassing us?"

"No son, don't utter their name now. It will just give you heartburn. They put the entire blame on your poor father. They separated him from his family. They ruined us. The thief is one of them, but they put the blame on your father. Goddess Ellamma is not blind to this. Thanks to her, the real thief was caught and everyone is witness. If you try to burn another's house, how can the fire not burn you? They knew the truth but blamed your father. We devote our labour to the patel and we have always trusted them. How can we steal from them? We have no guarantee that we will get paid for our labour, but we have never demanded an account of our wages. Can we be thieves? We, who know only hard work. They know all this, and yet they blame us. He was scared of being beaten to death, so he has gone god knows where. Shameless bastards. Not for nothing did the elders say that frogs have no tails and the kapu have no morals. Your father will give his life but not his pride."

"If he had heard that they had caught the real thief he may have come home by now. Don't know where he is or what he is doing ... no trace of him even after a year," Sangavva whined.

★

It kept raining that day. Even then, Mother swept the front of the house, plastered the ground with dung and cleared the rubbish. As she put the basket on her head and was about to cross the threshold, in walked my father. Mother cried out, "Look, children, your father is here!" We sat up. My younger brother ran up and held on to our father and began weeping. My elder brother and I went to him. He put the younger one on his shoulder, held the both of us and wept. In our happiness we stood rooted, taking him in from head to toe. Our Sangavva went in and brought water in a vessel, still weeping. Father took the water and put it next to him on the raised platform outside the hut. Mother started to put her basket down, but neighbour Ellavva called out saying, "It isn't auspicious to put a basket down as soon as you lift it ... walk a few steps, empty it out and come back." She ran to empty her basket, and then she and Sangavva sat down beside Father.

Sangavva started: "So many days, my son—where were you, what did you eat, what work did you do? You have turned into a black stick, my child. You have become half your size. Your wife, your children ... we have all been waiting for you like orphaned birds." She thought the better of going on like that, and said instead, "Whatever it is son, go wash your feet, quench your thirst, then we can talk."

Mother quickly took the jowar seeds to the flour mill, exchanged it for flour and began making hot rotte. My father ate his full and burped, saying, "How many days since I ate like this! Today I feel like I have eaten." He started telling us about his miserable life in the town. He had done all kinds of work. For a few days he worked as a construction labourer, then for a few days he waited at the adda. He even sold peanuts in a basket. With his wages he bought a spade and a crowbar. But then a police raid happened while he was waiting for work and he was charged with a fine. He sold his tools to pay it off and only then was he let go. He had left home with clothes on his body and came back in rags. Our Sangavva felt agonized just looking at my father. "Bad luck followed you from here to there." With her hand on his shoulder, she cursed, "May those tools and that town be brought to dust! What is lost is lost. You have come back, that is enough, son. Mother and children, all four of us will work hard together and we will not be slaves anymore." Father sat looking at the floor, running his fingers through the little one's hair.

Ningampalli Sayavva of the neighbouring keri came, asking, "How are you, Balappa?" Sayavva was holding a big cow-dung basket, two patched gunny bags and a worn-out yellow kunchi. Flies swarmed around her and she smelt of neem fruit. "If a person is alive, we will meet him some day. Only if he is buried will we never see him again. You have come back after so many days, my child. Where had you gone? They banished you to strange lands, those immoral people. Look here at the mother and the daughter-in-law ... your people. They looked after your land, they brought up your three children. Life has become a thorny fruit in these days of drought," said Sayavva to my father. He told her he had gone towards the town. Immediately, Sayavva said, "One of our own has returned to our fold. Work hard, live well ... as long as your arms are strong, you have life." As she said this, she turned to my mother and Sangavva: "Come on now, let's go quickly. You have three people in the house now, haven't you?" There were four working people in our house. My younger brother and I were the only ones who had to be fed. My elder sister was already married.

Mother poured thick gruel into a bowl, added a little salt and placed it in the groove of a wall for both of us. "If the dogs come and eat it, you will be hungry. Be careful, don't leave the doors open when you go play." They left to gather neem fruit in the forest, and after cleaning their yield in a pond, they dried the fruit and sold the seeds to Komati Narayana Shavukar on their way back. Then they bought food grains for the night like they did every day.

"This famine has come like Yama. People like us will survive only if the rains are good this year, otherwise a time may come when all of us will starve to death," my mother mumbled as she washed the pots.

"All these days we managed by feeding the children gruel. Now my son has come. The house is full of neem's bitterness. My mouth tastes like dry grass. Today we have gathered a few more neem seeds… We can buy salt, chilli, broken rice. Why not go to the butcher Ismail and buy a kilo of meat and make a curry?" grandmother said. Mother agreed.

They came back home with everything they needed. My younger brother and I were jumping with excitement. The little fellow didn't seem to need a reason to keep laughing. Watching us, my mother's face lit up. The satisfaction of being able to feed us to our heart's content that day was written all over her face. My younger brother hung on to the end of Mother's sari, playing the brat, saying, "Mother, a piece for me." So, my mother took a few pieces from the curry, threw them into the wood fire, and gave us a beautifully roasted piece each. She kept some aside for my elder brother. We came out to where our friends were and made their mouths water as we ate slowly, relishing our pieces of meat.

On one stove the meat curry was cooking and on the other the broken rice was boiling away. A mouth-watering aroma filled the house, spilling out over the threshold. Father came back from the bazaar, and sat on the platform outside. "Is your mother cooking meat? Such a wonderful smell." He called out to my mother, "Give me a little money, I feel like drinking toddy today." She said, "Where is the money left after buying salt, chilli and meat? It's all over." After some time, he said again in a loud voice, "You give me ten excuses when I ask for a little money to drink toddy." She said, "This is not fair … do you think I have hidden the money? You've seen everything. You know how things are … how can you still ask me for money?" Father pounced on my mother, "It's not fair? You've learnt to talk! What? Have I seen everything? How would I know what you have been doing?"

Mother went inside quietly and sat at the stove adjusting the firewood. "What? You, you! You don't say anything! I am asking you … what have I seen?" He kicked her hard on the back. My younger brother and I screamed. Father looked at us with menace in his eyes. Scared of him, we quietly hid in a corner. He beat her like she was cattle. She was wailing, saying, "Oh mother, I am dead, he'll take my life." But Father did not stop. I felt like I would die, watching my mother being beaten like that. My younger brother trembled and wet his pants. We did not have the courage to stop Father. We were scared that he might beat us too if we went near him. We were also scared that Mother might die.

Women on their way to the drinking water well gathered around our house on hearing the noise. They called out to my father. Finally, he stopped and walked out of the house. We went to Mother. She was lying so still. We could not wake her up. Then Sangavva came and started abusing Father. "Not even three days since you came back and you have started beating her up, you asshole. You have fallen like Yama on her! How much will you beat her? Look at the injuries all over her body. You have made her helpless. How do you think she will work? If you have the balls go show this anger to the people who called you a thief. When you left us to wander around the country, she looked after your children and me. Anyone else would have left us to our fate. She starved her own stomach to fill ours. She kept all those who cast their eyes on her at a distance and looked after this house, you jackass." Sangavva continued abusing him. All the women scolded, "Is this what you learnt in town … to beat your wife? All this while her eyes were sore, waiting for you to come back … and this is what she gets from you."

Just then, some of our relatives from the neighbouring village arrived. They brought the news that my elder sister had prematurely given birth. She had gone to the fields to work and had delivered there. Women in the fields helped her out and cut the child's umbilical cord with a sickle. They told us that they had taken the mother and the child home on a bullock cart. Both were doing well, they said. They had come to take my mother with them, immediately.

Our Sangavva broke into a cold sweat. "The child still had two more months left before it was time. How did it happen now? We thought of bringing her home for delivery. God had other plans. Tell me, my dear, are the mother and child doing well?" she asked again. Then Sangavva turned towards my father: "What will you do now, you shameless idiot? I gave birth to a good-for-nothing fellow. You have broken her back. Now who will wash your daughter's stained clothes? The tradition is that the mother should help at the first delivery. What shall I do now?" she cried, with her hand on her head.

Ningampalli Sayavva came forward and said, "What is the use of saying all this now? The new mother needs her mother to wash her soiled clothes. Did the elders say in vain that 'an elephant-like father may go, but the small basket-like mother should stay'?"

She told us to fetch some vayili leaves and massage mother's back with them to numb her pain. I went running towards the vayili tree.

TRANSLATED BY DIIA RAJAN

TRACE IT!

Jaada

Weddings and funerals—every member of every family has to attend these. This is the way of our village since god knows when. These are the ceremonies of life, and all the rites are conducted, participated in and followed keeping in mind every particular detail, because—well, that is the way of our village. Times are changing, and life has changed completely, but the way of our village has not changed. Except, maybe, a little. So, we are allowed to take some liberties here and there, but all the same, at least one member of every family in our village must attend every funeral and every wedding. That's that.

When someone in our village dies, every family sends a drummer. We are a wada of drummers and every drummer sent to a funeral must play his drum and throw in a fistful of earth into the deceased's grave as a sign of respect. They must.

Narsappa's daughter, Sukkamma, was related to everyone. Even when she grew old and her back grew crooked and she could not even see the glasses on her nose, she still considered the daughter of the whole village. It seemed like no one noticed that she was old, that was until the day she suddenly up and died. And in our village such news never went unnoticed or unmentioned. We heard about it from every member of every family.

"Oye! No work today," Narsappa cried out to the young man working on the other side of the road. "Go, go tell everyone, there is not going to be any work today."

"Old man, couldn't you have told us so any earlier? My father has already left for the bazaar," the young man retorted.

"If your father has left, how does it matter? You can come and play the dappu. Haven't you heard what I said? There is a dappu hanging on a hook in my house. Go get it, and you can play."

"Play? What will I do there with your dappu and old men like you? I can come and throw in a fistful of earth if you want." Youthfulness is usually not useful in these kinds of situations, and the boy's response irked the good Narsappa.

"You think you are a big guy, huh? That we don't drum half as well as you? Have you ever heard the sounds that rise from a practised hand? Play with us today and you'll know that even when a tiger grows old, his stripes don't fade. Did you learn to play the dappu by watching children play, or did you learn from a master who knows the nuances of his drum? Come today, and you'll learn from the very best."

"Are you challenging me, old man? Your dappu will only play as long as your bottles of toddy are not empty... After that both you and your dappu will be flat on the ground. Go find someone else. It would be more challenging to play kabaddi with trees than to play the dappu with all of you. I don't want to be the only person who is left to play in the end. Go find someone else."

"What are you saying? Who says you'll play alone? Bring your friends and tell them to bring their dappu too. Pentadu, Chandrudu, Sammadu, Nagadu, Guruvadu, Yelladu—call all of them, we will all go, and we will play till we drop. No one will have to play for anyone. Young and old, we will all play together and no one need be tired."

Babaiah was happy to go if his friends were coming. "Okay then."

Everyone was called and they left for the other village, their drums slung over their shoulders. They played the drums with gusto—dhoom dham—until the corpse was buried.

They lifted up coins with their sweaty foreheads to the rhythm of the dappu; they picked up needles stuck in the sand with their eyelids, keeping time with the drum. The funeral beat of fifty dappu thundered out the message of Sukkamma's death to ten surrounding villages. The women keened. The men born from her womb, and those born alongside her, wept like women, into their head-cloths. Crowds came to the funeral as if to a jatra. 'She came upon this earth and saw all, did all, she now takes leave of us all, our Sukkamma. Death must come like this. It is a good death,' they thought to themselves. 'She nursed her daughters and her daughters-in-law, but never troubled anyone herself. It is a death as good as gold,' people felt as they moved along in the wake. They plucked handfuls of tangedu flowers as they walked and strew them on her body as it lay in the burial pit. Each of them picked a fistful of earth and cast it in. Thus was she buried.

Finally, they sat down on one side and drank a bottle of toddy each. The younger ones did not drink, so they took money instead.

"Come, let's go to Ismail Hotel. We can eat bajji there." Pentaiah held out his hand to collect a share of everyone's money. They walked to the place where the bus might stop and the old and the young sat and waited, drinking their toddy and eating their bajji.

The bus arrived after some time, and one by one, the old men, the young boys and their dappu climbed in. They squeezed past the passengers, holding onto their dappu for dear life, crushing all and sundry as they hurried towards empty seats. But the bus had not plied even a mile before it sputtered and hushed to a stop. The driver and conductor walked around it, clicking their tongues at each other before one of them stuck his head into the bus and mumbled something about a mechanic. The driver and the conductor looked at each other, and simultaneously said, "It will take time." Then they nodded their heads at us.

What could we do? We also looked at each other and nodded our heads. Our dappu were still slung on our shoulders, and at least one of us was losing his patience.

"What the hell ... first some tea in the morning and then some toddy ... I've not had anything to eat or drink and it's making my body tremble. We are too weak to walk to the next village—and the one after that is even further. I think my stomach is going to eat me from the inside. What are we going to do, kids?" asked Narsappa.

But the young boys just looked at each other. There was nothing they could do. And what did the kids know anyway about what they could do. Slowly, one by one, they left in search of water—maybe there was a well around ... and then someone thought they spotted a ditch near a large banyan tree.

"Let's go and see," Avvola Nagaiah said, his words a query and a command.

They walked around and stopped at the ditch. It looked like there was only a tiny bit of water, and that too at the very bottom. Mostly, it was dry except for the leaf-green moss growing on the damp mud.

Pentaiah, Sendraiah, and Babaiah began digging into the mud with some sticks. First, two of them dug while the third one scooped the mud out. Then the third one dug and the first two did the scooping. Once the hole was a foot-deep, water began trickling into it from the bottom. It rose up to their wrists, and when all three of them had scooped enough mud out, more and more water seeped in. They plucked the nicest moduga leaves and gave them to Yellaiah, who folded them into small cups. Sammaiah and Guruvaiah scooped out the first of the muddy water with their little cups and threw it away, and when the ditch started to fill with shimmering clear water everyone dipped their cups in and drank.

"Come Narsappa," Pentaiah and Babaiah called out. "Come, drink this water and tell us if it is not sweeter than your toddy."

"Beev," they belched after drinking their fill and sat under the shade of the big banyan tree. In the meanwhile, Nagaiah had gone missing. "Where the hell did Nagadu go? Has he gone to take a leak?" Pentadu wondered aloud. "No, probably gone for the big job … he should be back," said Yellaiah, Babaiah agreed. "Yeah, looks like that."

"Did he take his dappu along or did he leave it with someone?" Pentaiah asked, looking around at the men holding on to their dappu. Everyone had only one dappu. "Looks like he's taken it with him. Can someone call out to him? The bus may be ready to leave now."

So Sammaiah began shouting "Oree Nagaaa! Nago! O…"

"Oi! What are you shouting out like that for, you fool … what's that dappu in your hand for? Can't you use it, shithead?" Babaiah nodded in agreement. And so Sammaiah started to call out with his dappu: "*Jagtak jagtak jagtak.*"

"*Jagintak, jagintak, jagintak*, I'm coming," Nagaiah called out almost instantaneously as he walked back to them. But the bus had still not been fixed.

"Looks like this is going to take a long time … shall we play a game?" Pentaiah asked. Everyone thought it was a good idea and the boys perked up immediately. "Who'll play the dappu?" Pentaiah looked around waiting for a response.

Yellaiah picked up his dappu hanging on the branch next to Babaiah. He stuck it under his arm, pulled out the stick tucked between its strings, and tested the drum: *tan tan*. It sounded fine. He took the german silver ring off his finger.

Pentaiah pulled the towel off Nagaiah's shoulder to tie it around Sammaiah's eyes. Yellaiah took Babaiah's ring and walked some twenty feet away towards a tangedu bush, placed the ring under the bush and covered it with a flat pebble. Blindfolded, Sammaiah would have to find the ring with the help of the beat from Babaiah's dappu.

Babaiah began. Sammaiah listened carefully. Everyone else watched. "Better play it right," Sammaiah warned the drummer. "Yeah, whatever…". He walked forward and the drum followed: *jadabuk-tak, jadabuk-tak*, telling him to keep walking, and so Sammaiah kept walking forward. As Sammaiah reached the tangedu bush the beat grew louder: *jadabuk-tak jadabuk-tak jadabuk-tak*. But when he walked past the bush, the beat changed instantly: *tan … tan … tan*. Sammaiah retraced his steps. But he was still walking away from the bush, so Babaiah changed the beat to *jagtak-ningtak, jagtak-ningtak*, urging Sammaiah to change direction. But Sammaiah continued to walk away from the bush. So *tana-nan tana-nan tana-nan*, Babaiah beat his drum, forcing Sammaiah to whirl around and walk towards the tangedu, but he was still walking in the wrong direction.

Asking him to slow down, Babaiah beat out *jaj-jeggu-tak jaj-jeggu-tak jaj-jeggu-tak*. Sammaiah slowed down. The dappu went *jejje-daaku jaggu-taaku* and he turned to the left. He stopped and listened carefully, wondering which way to move. Then he heard a *jadabuk-tak jadabuk-tak* and knew that he'd come closer. He took two steps forward, cautiously. He went down on his knees and looked for the ring with his hands. *Jadabuk-tak* said the dappu and Sammaiah scrambled forward for another couple of feet and fell forward on his knees. The boys laughed. Sendraiah ran up to Sammaiah to tighten the blindfold, which was coming loose. "Do it carefully, asshole, my eyes are burning … it's all dark," Sammaiah said. The dappu restarted, and to let him know that he was almost there, Babaiah beat a slow *jaggu-jaggu-tak ningu-ningu-takjaggu-jaggu-tak ningu-ningu-tak*. Sammaiah took small steps. When the rhythm changed to *tana-nan tana-nan tana-nan* he walked back a little, wondering where the ring was.

Then he heard a *jejje-daaku jaggu-taaku jejje-daaku jaggu-taaku*, took four small steps forward, stopped and looked around. The dappu changed its beat to *tana-nan tana-nan tana-nan* and he turned around again. *Jadabuk-tak jadabuk-tak*, the dappu told him to walk forward two steps. Then he heard *jadabuk-tak jadabuk-tak* again, and walked another couple of steps. When the beat changed to *tan tan tan tan* he knew he was almost there. So he started to feel the earth with his feet. The dappu changed the beat completely: *jaj-jeggu tak jaj-jeggu*.

Sammaiah had lost the plot and he was going to lose his cool with the drumbeats changing so swiftly and confusing him. But he didn't want to give up, so he called out "Arre play it properly … what shit are you playing, you…"

"You do your thing right, you asshole," replied Babaiah. "Go slow and think—stop chasing hens." *Tana-nan tana-nan*, beat Babaiah. Sammaiah slowed down and reached the tangedu. Then, *dan dan dan dan* the dappu changed again. Sammaiah started to search with his hands and feet. His hand found the tangedu and the dappu cued him with *dan dan dan* again. He slipped down onto the ground and began to feel the earth with his hands. He found the stone and the ring underneath it.

Now he must get back to the dappu, he thought to himself. His head was boiling and his ears were ringing. When he tried opening his eyes, he could only see the darkness of the blindfold. He stood up and listened carefully. The dappu called to him: *jadabuk-tak jadabuk-tak*. Sammadu walked forward, put the ring in Babaiah's hand and untied the towel from around his eyes. He'd won this round.

"Awesome … well done!" Everyone congratulated Sammaiah. "Then, what did you think of my brother?" asked Yellaiah. "My brother won and you lost … will you bring down a pot of toddy or climb onto a donkey?" he asked Pentaiah with a shameless smirk on his face. "Oi, shithead! When we started, did we say the loser would give everyone toddy or ride around on a donkey?" Pentaiah responded coolly.

"Don't pay any attention to him, he is just teasing you," said Nagaiah. "We didn't think about it, but when we get back home those who want their toddy will drink it and the rest will get something to eat. Come on, let's get back to the bus." They all headed back. "Anyway," continued Nagaiah, "wasn't it just the other day that Babugadu bought us all toddy after he winnowed his paddy? Poor chap, how can he buy us another round? He's got a hencoop full of children and only so much to feed them with. And it's only because he is so clever with his dappu that the ring was found. Otherwise, Sammadu would still be looking!"

"Come on, the bus is fixed, let's go," shouted out the conductor. They all piled in and the bus set off.

TRANSLATED BY DIIA RAJAN

BRAVEHEART BADEYYA

Madiga Badeyya

The madiga gudem is filled with sounds of 'tung, tung, tung'. It is the peak of summer, a difficult time to find wage work in the fields. During this season every household sends two or three people to get tangedu branches from the nearby forest for their leatherwork. Forty households engage themselves in the same kind of work. While the adults work in the house, the children play in the courtyard.

Enkayya and Ellamma had left for the forest before cockcrow to collect tangedu. They were back by lunchtime with two head-loads. Standing at the doorstep, they drank some rice water. Only then did they sit down on the verandah to catch their breath. Their eldest daughter Sammakka fetched rice and pulusu, raw tamarind soup with chopped raw onions and green chillies, in two bowls, and said, "Eat something now." Ellamma asked, "Where are your sisters and brothers, my child?" Enkayya rose immediately from where he had sat down to eat, calling out to his son, "Ori, Badeyyo!" There was no response to the first call. At the second call, Badeyya emerged, holding on to his bone-cart. He was breathless from having run so fast.

There is a particular fondness for Badeyya—not only in this house, but in the whole madiga gudem.

Badeyya is not the only name he has. His mother calls him by one name and father by another. But as he is the only one from the gudem who attends school—badi—the name Badeyya has stuck. His mother had named him after her brother Mysayya, who died of snakebite in the red gram fields. She was extremely fond of him. She wanted everyone to remember her brother every time her son's name was called out. His father named him Muthaiah because he was the last of the seven children and was as beautiful as a pearl—muthyam. So his mother calls him Mysayya and his father calls him Muthaiah. Uncles, aunts and other members of the community call him Badeyya.

Badeyya has always had a special talent for making toys. Whenever it was his father's turn to dispose of a dead animal in the village, Badeyya followed him until the animal's body was skinned. He got hold of the head to make a bone-cart, dried the skull, turned it over, chipped off a small piece from the centre, inserted a rope through the earholes, and the cart was ready. Then, two children pulled the two ends of the rope like two bullocks. They played 'load-the-cart'—loading the tiny cart with manure, and then unloading it in the fields.

But at school the teacher made Badeyya sit at the back of the classroom, on the floor. He thought that he would pollute the other students. Badeyya always listened to the teacher intently, did his homework without fail, and recited the lessons the next day. But because he was from the madiga caste, his place never changed from the back of the class.

Now as Badeyya's father calls out to him, his two brothers and sisters also come home, running. Everyone eats a little rice with sour curry and then gets busy with work. Enkayya goes to the adda—the usual spot in the corner of the street where he works every day. He carries all the necessary tools of his craft—leather, thread, thick needle, leather-beating tools, and a little water in a leather pouch. Ellamma gets busy with the tangedu branches that she has brought—piling them up to dry outside and taking out the yarn. Badeyya picks up his bone-cart, gathers the other children and goes out to play 'load-the-cart'.

The children have collected cow dung from the outskirts of the village and dumped it into small pits in the spaces between their houses to prepare manure. Unbeknownst to the children, their mothers use this raw dung with water to clean their front yards. On realizing that their dung has been stolen, the children keep watch and soon discover the thieves. Any urge to fight with their mothers is quickly put to rest when they are firmly warned that their fathers could be informed.

The children transport the dung from the small pits to the field in Badeyya's bone-cart. Outside the village, they prepare a field beside a path. They till the small piece of land with toy ploughs and make a boundary. Then they sprinkle it with jowar and rice seeds. But, alas! As people and cattle walk on it, the field is trampled into a path again. The adults feel sorry for them, "Ayyo! Land tilled with all this labour has got ruined."

They suggest, "Children, instead of sowing the seeds here, why don't you look for some other place where your labour will not go to waste?" All the children agree that this is worth taking seriously. They search for a patch of land and find it next to the drinking water well. They now start cultivating this piece of land.

★

There is no firewood at Badeyya's home to cook the evening meal. Ellamma asks her son, "Badeyya, why don't you come with me to gather some wood?"

He readily agrees. It is almost dusk and not much daylight is left. He wonders when they will be back if they start now. 'As it is,' he thinks, 'Avva suffers from night blindness. After dark she can't see and stays put in a corner. She needs my help for every little thing. How can she go now? Maybe if I go with her, we can quickly collect some firewood together. I can carry it on my head and both of us can get back home soon.'

"Let's go, Avva," he tells his mother. They take a rope to tie up the firewood and set out from home. They start gathering firewood from the red gram fields next to the village. Right at that moment, Ellamma sees Ramreddy Dora walking by. Seeing him, she swiftly removes her slippers and resumes work. The field is full of thorny bushes that poke at her feet. As if that is not enough, a long dry red gram stalk pierces her foot like a knife. Blood gushes out. She controls her pain and calls out to her son: "Badeyya, it is killing me."

Badeyya runs to his mother, pulls out the stalk, and squeezes some blood out. Running to the side of the field, he plucks some nallalam leaves, crushes them between his palms and applies it to the wound. He brings some water from the pond in a leaf-bowl for his mother to drink.

"Avva, you sit here. Let me collect some more wood and then we can go home with the pile."

Badeyya wears leather slippers. While he gathers the firewood in the fields, the thorns simply get crushed under his feet. Once he has enough wood, he ties it up in a bundle. Before lifting the pile onto his head, he helps his mother to her feet and looks out for her slippers. But they are nowhere to be seen. Suddenly he sees a dog chewing at them at a distance. The slippers are in shreds. Mother and son give up hope of getting them back and head home.

As she limps along, Ellamma starts lamenting, "This dora appeared like Yama, right when we were collecting firewood. I barely removed my slippers and my foot got pierced. See what happened! Now a dog has chewed them out. Isn't that dog's life better than mine, Badeyya? As madiga, it is our work to make slippers. Your father makes slippers for all the small and big castes in the village. Our slippers shield their feet from mud, stones, thorns, twigs, poisonous creatures and everything else. Even when they go to the moon they wear our slippers, don't they? I am born in the caste that makes slippers for everybody, but my own feet are left bare. Let me sit for a while."

Badeyya helps her sit down. His mother's words have left him saddened. They keep ringing in his ears. How swiftly she had walked when they started for the fields, and now she has collapsed in pain. Unable to contain himself any longer, Badeyya asks his mother a question that has always bothered him, "Why do you always have to remove your slippers when the dora walk by?"

"Badeyya, do you think they'll keep quiet if I don't remove my slippers? Even when they look as if they have not noticed anything, they keep it in mind and vomit it out some other time. Do you think we can live if we offend them? This pain will disappear tomorrow. The snake has poison in its fangs; the scorpion in its tail; but the dora are poison all over. They keep their vengeance alive till they die. To fight them, we need caste, power and land. We have neither the caste nor the power. If we have to gain that power, caste has to go."

It is dark now. Avva is not able to see because of her night blindness. A hundred thoughts race through Badeyya's mind as he balances the pile of firewood with one hand and holds his mother's hand with the other. "How will she manage when she goes to the forest tomorrow morning for the tangedu branches?"

One thought calms him down.

On reaching home, he secretly takes the leather hidden by his father in the shelf and soaks it in the clay barrel under the tamarind tree. Everybody falls asleep after dinner, but not Badeyya. His heart is in the leather, soaking in the barrel. He gets out of bed right after midnight, takes the leather out and picks up the shoemaking tools from his father's bag. First, he cuts out enough leather for slippers. Then he takes the measurement of his mother's foot; cuts the leather to the measure of the sole, the toes, and the rest of the foot. He sews the slippers; puts nails on them; then he polishes them. He has made a new pair of slippers for his mother. He thinks they may not look as good as the ones his father makes, but surely they would be useful when Avva goes to the forest the next morning. Placing them safely on the shelf, he goes to sleep.

Everyone wakes up in the morning as usual. Enkayya tells his wife, "How will you come to the forest with the wound on your foot? Stay at home." Through the night, Ellamma's children have taken turns to nurse her, applying a warm poultice of medicinal leaves to her foot. It feels a little better now, though she is still weak. However, she insists on going with him. "No. How can I stay home without doing any work? I want to come but I'll need slippers. And why don't you arrange for some medicine for my night blindness?"

"I can make new slippers for you; just give me a day or two. I cannot do much about your night blindness though. I've been telling you that if you patiently go around our neighbourhood begging, and eat the food given to you for three weeks, you'll be cured. You never listen to me."

"Let your begging idea go to hell. I feel terrible doing that."

"Why? Are you begging from strangers? Are you asking people from other castes? You are only going to our madiga. They are our own kith and kin. Why should you feel bad about it?" Enkayya tries to placate Ellamma. "Since you don't have slippers today, why don't you wear mine?"

Badeyya wakes up to the sound of his parents talking. As his father begins to take off his slippers, he says, "Bapu, Avva has her own slippers. Why are you taking yours off?" Badeyya brings out the new slippers and places them at his mother's feet. Both his parents are taken by surprise. "Where did you get these slippers from?" they ask.

"I made them," Badeyya says proudly, his voice brimming with pride and happiness.

Unable to believe what they are seeing, both Enkayya and Ellamma say in unison, "You have done such a wonderful job!"

Enkayya says in a voice full of joy, "Now that your son has made you new slippers, why don't you wear them?"

"Why wouldn't I? Do you think you are only one who can make slippers? My Muthaiah is no less than you. He is a mountain of gold, he is! You don't need to teach him. He learns simply by watching."

Ellamma can't stop praising Badeyya. After returning from the forest, she tells everyone in the village about his achievement, "Look, my youngest son has made these new slippers for me. Look, he simply watches and learns! Look!"

TRANSLATED BY A. SUNEETHA

BUT WHY SHOULDN'T THE BAINDLA WOMAN ASK FOR HER LAND?

Baindlame Bhumadagada Mari?

Wherever people gathered or met in the wada of the village, they asked, "Why does the dora keep saying the baindla woman banged her fist on the table? She didn't do it for nothing. It was only to ask for her rightful land."

★

It was still dark, the light just a glimmer. You couldn't make out who was coming towards you. The women were busy sweeping their courtyards and coating the floor with cow-dung slurry. The men went 'herre! herre!' prodding the cattle awake while they cleaned out the sheds. Others prepared to harness the oxen and assemble the ploughs. One by one the women drifted towards the well carrying their pots for water.

'Bantu' Pentappa came up running pell-mell, holding up the 'servant' staff.

"What's the big hurry, Pentappa? You're running as if your life depends on it. You'll trip on stones in the dark and fall," chided Madiga Dunnolla Narsamma.

"Amma, I've to give this message to the sarpanch and rush off," Pentappa said without breaking stride. "Is Sarpanch Balappa awake? Please wake him up."

"What are you saying? Do you imagine that he is still curled up and sleeping?" the sarpanch's wife retorted.

"Ya, ya, I know he is already busy ploughing the fields! But tell me, is he up?"

"He's gone to the fields with the farm-servant to start the ploughing." Saying this, she got busy with the decorative skirting she was creating on her front wall.

"I couldn't catch him despite coming so early. Amma, please send one of the children to tell him that the dora wants to see him immediately. Tell him I came personally. I still have to tell the caste elders." Pentappa wound up his turban again so that it sat more tightly round his head and hastened off.

Morning had still not fully broken when, on hearing from 'Bantu' Pentappa, the caste elders along with the sarpanch gathered at the dora's house. They all sat in their places waiting for him.

Finally, by noon, the dora came out holding the tail of his lungi in one hand. As if on cue, the other big men—Krishna Reddy Patel, Srinivas Rao Pantulu, Narasimha Reddy and Anantha Reddy Patel—entered.

All the seated elders stood up, removed their turbans, tucked them under their arms and paid obeisance to the dora with folded hands. The five patels then settled onto the chairs placed a few feet away.

The dora, Narender Reddy, began speaking: "Orey Saiga, Yelliga, Malliga, Naga—listen carefully. Let me tell you what happened last night. Ooradamma appeared in my dream and said, 'I'll destroy the village; I'll create havoc. If the village is to prosper, I have to prosper. I want a sacrifice. My sisters Mysamma, Pochamma, Raktamysamma, Bangaramma, Eedamma—are all famished. You have to satisfy them with a gift of seven he-goats. Otherwise, I will bring down a pox on your house and everyone in your family will die a painful death.' She didn't allow me a wink of sleep the whole night. What shall we do?"

"Let us call the erpula woman, the baindla man, and Pothuraju Sayigadu, and consult them. We should make sure that, somehow or the other, we conduct the festival this year and make sacrifices to please the Goddess," said Srinivas Rao Pantulu.

The dora ordered 'Bantu' Pentappa, "Go, get the erpula woman first. Let's see what she has to say about when it should be held. Hurry!"

The servant hurried off. He had only gone a little distance when he came across some friends.

Looking important, Pentappa said to them, "Orey, Ooradamma came into the Patel's dreams last night and told him to hold a jatra in the village … or else! So I think we're going to have the Ooradamma festival this year. They've told me to go fetch Baindla Saayamma. That's where I am headed."

He got to Baindla Saayamma's house and said, "Saayamma, the Patel has asked you to come. I don't know why."

"This does not happen often. Why's he asking for me? Don't try to tell me you've come without knowing why. You must know something. Tell me. He won't eat you up if you do. I'll come only if you tell me… I'm busy right now. Go away," she said decisively.

"What do I know, Amma? Do they tell me everything? It seems Ooradamma appeared in his dreams. We have to hold the jatra and he asked me to fetch you. This is what I learnt and I don't know anything more."

"You could have told me all this right at the beginning. Okay, let's go. Yelluga, bring brother Ramsendra along to the Patel's house," Saayamma said and walked out of the courtyard.

★

"Greetings, Patel. You've thought of me after a long time."

"Saayamma, when did we ever forget you? You people have been conducting the festival since your grandfather's time. During my grandfather's time, your grandmother did it. It was the same during my father's time. And so it continues. Come, sit down. Have your brothers come? Did you call them?" asked the patel.

"Yes, I did. Look, they have arrived," said Saayamma.

"Is it enough if your brothers come? Where are the palodu, edurupalodu and avathalodu? Don't you have to call them as well?"

"What's the problem, Patel? Send for them if you want them."

"Arrey! Go tell that pali-baindla fellow also to come."

"I'm here," Baindla Anthappa called out from the back. He had wrapped a blanket around himself.

"Hey, Antiga! We don't see you much these days! Are you people still together or is it everyone for themselves now? It's better to find out right at the beginning," the patel queried.

"Aah, Patel! What's there that you don't know? We're all together. Whatever festival we conduct, we share what we get equally—be it debts or earnings. Ramaiah, why are you not saying anything?"

"Why do you need to ask me? As if you are saying something that's not true? Yes Patel, we're all together," said Ramaiah.

"When did you all become so united? Just the other day you were breaking each others' heads. You tricksters can't be trusted. Anyway, since you say you are united, let's get to the point. I had a dream last night and I want to realize it. All the important people of the village are here. The caste elders are here, the erpula woman is here, the pothuraju is here. All we have to do is talk and come to an agreement. We've decided to have the Ooradamma jatra. What do you say? This is the time to clear your doubts and share your opinions."

"What's there to. say? This is for the whole village, so everyone has to contribute money, and the festival must be conducted in a fine manner. All the neighbouring villages have held their festivals. It is my desire that our village should also do so this year, and I am offering a male buffalo calf from my herd for the sacrifice," said Patel Narasimha Reddy.

"Yes, what the Patel says is right. I also have a male calf and will give it in the name of Ooradamma," said the patwari, Srinivasa Rao Pantulu.

"That's already two. I'll offer a bull to Ooradamma," said another reddy.

It was decided that each household from the mala, madiga, golla, mangali, eediga, chakali and besta communities would give four seers of rice each. In addition, each of the sabbanda elders would contribute a he goat.

"Okay. No one should come in the way of good deeds. One from the pantulu, one from the dora, two from the patel and five from the sabbandollu. That makes nine, all told. Tomorrow we'll bring all the animals in a procession to the temple, to the accompaniment of drum-beats, and let them loose in the village. So everything's settled. Make sure that all the drummers come tomorrow morning at nine to the Ooradamma temple. Is there anything else we need to talk about?"

"Only the erpulamma's issue. Once we discuss her payment, we'll be done. So what do you say, erpulamma?"

"Look, Patel. Can I bring up past issues also or should I stick to the present festival?" Erpula Saayamma asked.

"This is a festival. A big festival. Why should you restrict yourself to the present festival? Go ahead, ask for your other dues too."

"The last time we had the Ooradamma festival in our village, instead of calling me you got the erpula woman from the neighbouring village to conduct it. This time you are asking me, but not even bringing up the issue of the manyam land I'm entitled to."

"Now Saayamma, don't go on about that. First, just tell us whether you want to be the erpula woman for this village or not," the pantulu said angrily.

"I do. But first tell me about my land. Earlier, when my paternal aunt used to perform the ritual function, the Nizam Sarkar gave her three acres of land. Now, that land has been taken over and is being cultivated by one of your cousins. You've to get that land returned to me."

The dora didn't expect her to be so brazen, openly asking about the land encroached upon and being cultivated by his cousin.

"You shouldn't talk so loosely, and that too in front of everyone," he admonished her, struggling to keep a calm front. "We'll talk about this tomorrow," he said and turned to talk to the patwari.

The caste elders gestured Saayamma to go away, indicating that the dora might really lose his temper if she continued to stand there. Saayamma prepared to leave.

"If we give her the slightest chance to talk, she starts digging up things from the past. She doesn't allow anyone else to intervene. The problem is, she does not know her place and doesn't know how to talk to her superiors," the dora said, looking at the others expectantly as if wanting them to confirm what he had said.

"Really, Narender! What guts she has. Saying your man is cultivating her land. Where did this woman get the land from? Who gave it to her? Even if she suspects something, how dare she speak so openly? It's really your fault, being so lenient with all of them," said Patel Krishna Reddy. "These baindla people are all the same. Just let them get a word in and they will eat up your head. You should always make sure they stay in their place. If you give them so much as a foothold, they'll take over the house. See now, all you do is ask them to perform the erpula's role in the Ooradamma festival and they start talking about land … do they think land comes for free or that the wind brings it? Why do these riff-raff need land?"

"No, Reddy. There's a lot to be done, and we cannot get frustrated over such little things. Let's drink some tea and think through this problem coolly. We'll give these people bidis to smoke and ask them to sit outside and wait," the Karnam Pantulu said, placating the dora.

Everyone felt much less tense after a round of tea. Then the karnam began. "If we scold this erpula woman, she may refuse to come, like she did last year. We have to sweet-talk her into performing the rituals and the soothsaying. Also, there are other things linked to this issue. If she makes a fuss, it will affect the madiga, and then the sabbanda. In your anger you are forgetting how many connections this woman has. We should remember what the brahman purohit said—these village goddesses are not really part of the real Hindu tradition. If there are goddesses, they are only Lakshmi, Gayatri and Saraswati. These—Ooradamma, Mysamma, Pochamma, Ellamma and so on—we don't have them. These mala-madiga and the sabbanda—only they worship such deities and we should let them. But if we don't do all that is required on our part for this Ooradamma's festival, people will think that your dream is a lie and stop believing you. What is more, the elders will not give the animals they have pledged. There is also this other thing ... though we should keep this in confidence." Lowering his voice conspiratorially, he continued, "This is a tradition that is handed down from our ancestors and we should maintain it without compromise. We've to divert the deity's anger from us to the animals we're going to sacrifice. This is also the time to test how much the other castes in the village, specially the lower ones, are in our control. Keeping all this in mind, we have to conduct the affair with some foresight and make sure that everything happens smoothly."

They called in the elders and the erpula woman again. Addressing Saayamma, the Karnam Pantulu began, "Saayamma, to tell you the truth, in those days your aunt did not have any land, nor did she purchase any. If there was any such thing the record would be with the karnam. After my grandfather and father, I've been doing that job. If there were any record, wouldn't I let you know? Look, you are our village erpula woman. Wouldn't I want to help you? I help the whole village; I even help neighbouring villages. But the fact is that at that time your aunt didn't have any land ... and today you don't have any land. How can you ask for the village records? That is not at all the proper way to proceed."

"No, Pantulu. The village elders have all seen my aunt cultivate the land. I have the receipts of the taxes she has paid. And I inherited the erpula duties from her. She was my erpula guru and I am the successor to both her profession and her property."

"Look here, you're asking for your aunt's land, but you also say you do not want to perform the rituals. Yet you claim that you belong to this village. How's this possible?"

"Dora, I'm not saying I won't perform the erpula rituals. If you give my land back to me, the produce will feed my children. What I'm saying is that if you give me my aunt's land, I'll surely conduct the festival."

"Now, look here..." the dora stopped her roughly, but thought the better of it and continued more calmly: "Amma, whenever you open your mouth, you keep saying 'land, land, land'. Let me say this to your face. Your aunt did not have land and you do not have land. Conduct the erpula ritual if you want to, otherwise forget it. If you perform the rituals, do it for a payment ... if you do the soothsaying, do it for a payment. I don't want to hear all this stuff about land. Do you think the festival will stop if you say you won't come? Will we cut our own throats just because the knife is golden? Do you think there is no one else we can call? We will bring the erpula woman from Kotapally or Chintakunta. The festival will take place come what may."

"Why do you speak as though I am a wage-worker? I'm a daughter of this village. How can you treat me like a coolie? Was I not born here? How am I a coolie? My aunt's land is mine. I want that land, and only that. That's all. This village—

all of you together—made me a jogini. From the times of my ancestors, the girls of my family have been forced to become erpula. To deny me the land that is already in my name, you are trying to turn me into a coolie! Did I conduct these festivals all these years only to be insulted like this?" As she said this, all of Saayamma's many painful experiences flashed through her mind. The hardship she faced in raising and educating her children; getting her elder daughter married. You couldn't wish such hardship even on your enemies. All the anger and torment pent up in her stomach burst into flames and overwhelmed her. These dora and patel—what disgusting people they were. Earlier she had treated them with respect since they were dora. She had thought naively, 'These people who made me a jogini will look after my welfare.' Now they all seemed like poisonous creatures to her.

Saayamma, who had been controlling her anger so far, walked up and glared at the dora.

There was a dark, brooding silence. Everyone was waiting to hear whether she would agree to a wage. The dora, the patel and the sabbanda waited anxiously for something to happen. Baindla Saayamma spoke: "Dora, don't pay me coolie wages. Just give *your* daughter away as a jogini. Tell her to do the soothsaying during the festival. *I* will pay her the wages." Saying this, Saayamma pounded the table in front of the dora with her fist.

The dora's eyes popped out and his mouth fell open. The same thing happened to the Karnam Pantulu and the other patel men. Their mouths dried up and they fell silent. Time seemed to stand still. The sabbanda were all agog, thinking that Saayamma was going to grab one of those big men by the collar and drag him down. The crack of a tree trunk breaking in a high wind somewhere startled them. The thunder came crashing. Saayamma took one more step forward. The patel-folk stood transfixed, aghast at what was happening.

The sabbanda elders at the back rushed forward saying, "Amma … Amma … please stop, Saayamma," and tried to come between her and the dora. She pushed one of them on the chest with her palm and he fell backwards. One who can push away a man with such strength is no ordinary Saayamma; surely she must be possessed by Ooradamma herself! This is the work of Ooradamma, they all thought. As if unconsciously, all the patel paid obeisance to her, their palms joined in salutation. The Ooradamma who appeared to Narender Patel in his dream was already making good on her threats. A thunderous look appeared in Saayamma's eyes. She looked like a cheetah walking on burning embers. Everyone looked beseechingly at Saayamma's brothers. They pushed Pothuraju Sayappa forward. The five brothers got hold of her and tried to pull her back.

She glared at them defiantly.

★

Saayamma was the only girl in a family of boys and she had been raised with a great deal of affection. She had grown up without a care; her baindla family looked after her like she was a princess. She played with children from the madiga, mala, eediga, kummari, kammari, mudiraju, golla and chakali communities. Her mother often couldn't find her at mealtimes. Her brothers would have to search for her in the other neighbourhoods and bring her back so that her mother could cosset and feed her.

In keeping with the family tradition, they made her a jogini. But her maternal uncle freed her so that, unlike in other villages, she didn't have to become the wife of the village. Her family was prosperous, owning eight acres of fertile land. She had strong brothers who supported her with great affection. People from the other artisan communities addressed the baindla family as 'brother', 'sister', 'sister-in-law', and 'aunt', and had a friendly and respectful relationship with them. Saayamma had lived her life like the daughter of the village.

In due course, she gave her heart to Mudiraju Sendrappa. Her parents got her married to him and brought him to live with them. Then a domestic routine took over—children, their education and so on. All of a sudden, Sendrappa died.

They took the corpse from the baindla house to the mudiraju house and laid it out there. Saayamma's children keened and mourned near the body. The mudiraju also wept along with Saayamma, sharing her grief. No one knows exactly what happened, but after some time the village servant came and whispered something in the mudiraju people's ears. Their faces changed. Unaware of what was happening, Saayamma continued to weep. Her mother and sisters-in-law were trying to comfort her.

Then the mudiraju elder came up to Saayamma and said, "Saayamma, don't fall on the corpse and weep here. Go outside and weep. Go." The humiliation caused by his words pierced through her, adding to the sorrow she was already feeling. How had she suddenly become an untouchable while all this time no one had thought of it?

"If his wife does not sit near him and weep, where else will she cry? If he'd thought he was so high caste, why did he marry her? After he had three children, and after he died, this issue of untouchability comes alive with the corpse! How can that be?" the madiga elder Nagappa said.

Once again the mudiraju instructed Saayamma to leave the house, this time more firmly. Hearing that they were preventing Saayamma from grieving near her husband, the youth from the mala, madiga and baindla houses quickly gathered in the front yard of the mudiraju house. "Who is the bastard who has stopped her from grieving?" they asked. The elders restrained them, asking them not to create a disturbance near the corpse.

"'Get out of the house. Go outside and weep.' Why do we have to suffer the humiliation of listening to such things? Let's take the corpse and go back to our place," the madiga women consoled Saayamma.

"Let's pick up the corpse. Come on." The madiga and baindla men hitched up their dhotis and wound their turbans more tightly.

"How can you take him? He was born into this caste. We have to perform the rites and rituals. When he was alive, we never opposed him. Now it is our duty to bury him. The father has to perform the last rites," said the mudiraju elders.

"He has a wife and children. How can his father do the rites?"

Arguments were getting sharper between the madiga and the mudiraju.

"Why should we discuss all this with them? We are higher and they are lower in caste. She was not made a wife by the caste. She's only a mistress."

"Let's go. Let's go." The madiga group moved out and joined up with the madiga youth.

Seeing this, Saayamma said, "Why should all of you get so upset for my sake? I don't want this corpse and I don't want their caste. Come, my brothers, we should not utter a single word." She requested them with folded hands, "Let them not allow me to perform the last rites. Let them not allow me to weep. Let them keep the corpse if they want. Come!"

Everyone cooled down except for the madiga and baindla women who suddenly began to wail. Like a procession they wended their way through the mala houses, the madiga houses and finally arrived at the baindla houses. They made an effigy of a corpse with cloth and laid it out in the room. They lit a lamp near the head. In the night, they told funeral stories. The madiga brought their drums. The baagar dug the grave. They buried the effigy in the burial ground of the madiga. The whole village thought that the baindla people had observed the proper rituals.

★

Saayamma's father walked up unsteadily, leaning on his staff, and lovingly smoothed back her hair. He tied up her loosened hair into a knot and sprinkled some cold water on her face. He placed a turmeric bottu on her forehead and said to his sons, "Take your sister home." The strapping Yellappa hoisted his sister on to his shoulders and began walking home. Though her face had been sprinkled with cold water, her heart was smouldering and her innards were on fire…

"I'll see how you get this done by paying wages, you bastards! If you don't vacate my land, I'll sacrifice you. Only then will the curse be lifted from this village," she declared loudly from her brother's shoulder. He carried her away against her will.

The dora, the patel and pantulu heaved a sigh of relief. They looked at the caste elders and said, "How dare the baindla woman bang her fist on the table and talk legalities while all you buggers just stood and stared? Are you men, or do you wear bangles?"

"Fuck your mother ... wife ... you bastards ..." said the dora, trembling with rage. Karnam Pantulu and Komati Narayana interjected: "Dora, there is no use getting angry. It's no use wasting time scolding these people. We should focus on the festival that has to be held." They signalled to the elders to leave.

TRANSLATED BY SASHI KUMAR

JAMBAVA'S LINEAGE

Jambava Munum

In the madiga wada, Ellamma leaps into the air. Her face is fierce. Mothers pull their saris over their babies' frightened eyes and pat their backs to reassure them. Mother Ellamma grows fiercer. This time she throws herself on the ground. The chindu troupe sings, coaxing her to rise and sit up. She opens her eyes … but no, she is possessed again.

Pothuraju follows Ellamma carrying the whip-like eeragola. He recites the nudugulu as he performs. He breaks open coconuts and cuts up lemons. He casts the lemon bits onto Ellamma's head to exorcise her. But it has no effect. The drumming builds up to a crescendo. Pothuraju lifts the eeragola off his shoulder and lashes the air with it. It looks as though he is searching for someone or something in the crowd. His eyes rest on Golla Mallanna who is moving around in the front, carrying a lamb wrapped in a blanket. Pothuraju walks up to him, bites into the lamb's neck with his bare teeth, and then circles Ellamma. She grows calm. They wash her face with toddy.

The potters, the toddy-tappers, the shepherds, the washerpeople and the barbers set out from the madiga wada. They walk past the blacksmith neighbourhood. Accompanied by the caste elders, they reach the pedestal of the Ooradamma temple at the centre of the village and pause to pay respects to the deity who protects the village. Then everyone—children, women and men—walks in a procession towards the village tank. They are accompanied by drums. It feels like a festival. When they reach the tank, Mother Ellamma stops at the bund to visit her younger sister, Katta Mysamma. Then she enters the water. The first to enter the water after her is neeradayana —the person who irrigates the landlord's fields. Wetting his hand in the tank, he pays his respects to Ellamma by circling a burning oil lamp in front of her as mangalaharati and offering a 'dowry' that includes blouse pieces, coconuts and betel leaves. He carefully washes the paint off her face with water from the tank. Accompanied by drums, the villagers lead her into the tank, casting neem branches into the water before she enters it. Mother Ellamma blesses them. Then she emerges from the tank and walks up the bund. The elders of the sabbanda castes and other people from the village who were waiting on the bund now step into the water and wash their faces. Some of them take a full dip. Then they return to the village. "Poligoliga"—may the harvest be good—a shout goes up at the spot where Pothuraju bit into the lamb's neck. "Salaam poligalugani," the crowd responds in chorus. They climb down the bund and stop at the pandiri erected at the entrance-stone of the village to give thanks. The troupe blesses the village:

May you be blessed with good luck!

May your crops and cattle flourish!

May the children's lives be protected!

Salaam, poligalugani!

The troupe then circles the village and arrives at the madiga elder's house, where they sit down.

The Nizamabad Chindu Ellavva Troupe has a reputation across the country. The performers are of all ages and include women, men and children. Ellamma and Saayanna are the chief performers.

Ellamma speaks to the madiga elder: "The big event is over. The smaller event remains." By the time she has finished speaking, two cases of toddy, which the elder had exchanged for the two bags of paddy kept ready for this purpose, have arrived. The madiga of the troupe drink it together. This is the main remuneration they will receive. They cook the sacrificed goat and enjoy the meat.

That night the troupe sleeps in the madiga wada.

Next morning, they go into the village to work out their programme and agree on payments with the sabbanda caste elders. First, the elders pay their respects to Ellamma by touching her feet. She places her hands on their heads and blesses them saying, "Live peacefully, my children." Then, she begins the negotiations. Through song, the chindu troupe begins convincing the sabbanda caste elders that one performance should be sponsored by the village as a whole; besides, every caste could separately sponsor a performance. Both groups bargain hard. Ellamma reminds them that if the chindu perform in the village, there will be a good harvest. How could they not sponsor the performances?

★

While the troupe was inside negotiating, children and others crowded around outside. A group of youngsters—from the upper caste houses located in the south of the village—walked towards the chindu children. From the other end, another group of youngsters from the shepherd and toddy-tapper communities came up to them. The latter greeted the chindu respectfully, with folded hands. The upper-caste group stared at them as though something strange had taken place. But they did not stop with that. "Why is it necessary to salute them like that?" they asked.

To this, Golla Maddileti replied, "Because the stories they tell are our stories. They are *our* chindu. They perform the legends of Mandayechhu and Beerappa, both of which are stories of the shepherds. They tell the story of Pandavas to the mudiraju, and for the fisherfolk they perform Gangakalyanam, Pramilarjuneeyam and Balanagamma. They are talking about all this with the caste elders inside."

"What did you say, useless fellow? Did we hear you say 'they are our chindu?' You are shepherds, we're velama. They are madiga chindu. How dare you greet them so respectfully?" Velama Jalpati Rao shouted from the crowd. Chindu Cina Ellamma and Saraiah, who were listening in on this exchange attentively, felt disturbed. Cina Ellamma wondered: "Why do the velama respond like this while the rest of the village is so welcoming?" Not wanting trouble and not knowing what to say, she remained silent. The ruckus continued for some time.

It seemed as if they had come to an agreement inside. The elders of the troupe came out chanting: "May the cattle, the crops and the children flourish and may everyone live a happy life." The children who had been quietly waiting under the neem tree, their faces tense, stood up and joined them. Then the whole group walked together to meet the elders of the masons, potters, washerpeople, barbers, weavers, dudekalollu, toddy-tappers and discussed which stories were to be told and on which days. When they had finished, it was already time for the morning meal.

The troupe moved in a group to the washerpeople's neighbourhood. Each of them went into one of the houses. They were given some rice and koora to go with it, which they sat together and ate. They then moved to the madiga area, stopping at the madiga elder's house to rest in the padsaala in front of the house where he met guests. Ellamma pulled out her betel leaf bag. She went over and sat next to Cendravva, the madiga elder's wife, who was cleaning out the sand and stones from some paddy. There was a lot of rubbish because it was leftover paddy gleaned from the field after the harvest had been taken by the upper castes.

"Did you manage a good deal?" Cendravva asked Ellamma.

"Yes. We did. By the way, I don't have any kasu with me. Would you let me have some?" Saying this, Ellamma took out sunnam kayalu from her betel leaf bag and began dressing a betel leaf for each of them. She offered one to Cendravva continuing, "When the harvest is good the village is usually wholehearted about giving paddy to people like us, the labouring–singing people." Even as she was speaking to Cendravva while she chewed the leaves, her gaze kept returning to Cina Ellamma. She had noticed that the children were upset about something. She waited for an appropriate moment to ask them what was wrong. Now that she had chewed on her betel leaves, she felt more relaxed.

"Hey, children! What happened? Why are your faces so sad and shrunken? On other days you pester me for betel leaves. Why is there no such demand today? Here, take this leaf and chew it … it'll make your mouth turn red. I've put in some extra kasu," Ellamma said, trying to cheer them up and wheedle them into speaking. Cina Ellamma slowly moved closer. Putting her arm around the young girl's neck, Ellamma pushed back the hair from her face tenderly and pulled her close. "What happened my girl, why are you so upset?" she asked gently. Placing a betel leaf in her palm she asked again, "Tell me my child, what was it that happened?"

"They … they … treated us …" Cina Ellamma began.

"Who?" asked Ellamma.

"You were speaking to the shepherd elders inside … and we were sitting outside," Cina Ellamma began. Saraiah took over and detailed the whole sequence of events.

Oh! I didn't realize that so much happened while we were inside, Ellamma thought to herself. But she hid her anger. At some point the children have to learn about such things, she decided. This may well be the moment.

In the past, she too had been troubled on several occasions by such misbehaviour by upper caste people. But despite everything that she had to face, she had continued to perform, saving the art and culture of the Chindu Bhagotam from dying out. These children would also become great artistes. They need to know everything—there is no escaping this, thought Ellamma. Cina Ellamma and Saraiah sat opposite her, chewing their leaves and wondering what she was going to say.

Ellamma remained silent, wondering where to start. But the children were impatient. They plied her with questions. "People from the sabbanda castes speak of us as 'our people'. They say 'our chindu people'. They ask us to recite their legends. They bathe our deity Ellamma's face in the tank with respect. But why don't these people who believe that they are superior castes—brahman, velama, reddy—treat us the same way? You make us narrate their legends too. Don't ever ask us to do so again. They insulted me. 'You girl, come with me,' one of them said. My whole body burned with anger: 'Bastard, where to?' I asked. He glowered back at me angrily; threatened me. I just moved away.

"When we perform the Chindu Bhagotam we do so boldly, in front of the whole village. Why did he make me feel so ashamed that I had to move away?" asked Cina Ellamma innocently. Ellamma listened carefully. Cina Ellamma's young face was full of questions. Experiences born out of adversity give rise to wisdom and knowledge, Jambavathatha had said philosophically. Ellamma could see that Cina Ellamma had been deeply hurt and that she would not just accept things without protesting. It was time now for her to gain a deeper understanding of village life.

Ellamma began by talking about her own experiences in order to offer the young girl some strength. "My child, we too have lived through many similar experiences ... but we have somehow managed to keep the art of the Chindu Bhagotam alive. Those who resent or dislike us may speak harshly. We have to deal with them, persuade them maybe, but make sure that we continue with our own work. What you saw happening today is nothing compared to the high-handedness of the dora folk in the villages when I was a young girl. They would make us do all the work, and then say 'keep your distance ... you son of a madiga ... chinduloda ... dakkaloda.'

"Theirs was an uncivilized world, one that knew no humanity. All we knew then was suffering and misery. We were not allowed to live like human beings. In the villages as well as in the towns, those who owned large lands enjoyed power. We had to address them all—brahman, velama, reddy, kapu, karnam, Muslim nawabs—as dora! Had to bend and salute them. Work for them without wages. There was no way we could ask to be paid. If we did, they would mutter: 'These madiga and mala are getting uppity…' That's how it was. Even today we continue to struggle—for the sake of the sabbanda community and to protect the art of the Chindu Bhagotam. Like the eagle swoops down to carry away the chickens, they have swooped down and taken away the land, the air, the water, our work and our tools. And along with these, our play, our song and our art. Only the sabbanda still rely on us and on our art. We must protect our connections with them.

"The upper castes have turned all art into commerce; they make films, sell tickets and loot people. We never do that. When the sabbanda farmers get a good harvest, they offer us some of it happily and we accept it happily. When they get a bagful, they give us a measure from that. From their own plates, they give us a share of the food. And we share their problems. When we perform, it is for the sake of the sabbanda community, not just for their money. We need to think a little deeply about everything, my child! We should not get upset over these things or take them to heart. We must carry on the responsibility handed down to us by our Jambavathatha."

As they listened to Ellamma, Cina Ellamma and Saraiah fell silent. Something touched them deep inside and made them serious. After a while, Cina Ellamma said, "You're right, aunty. They trust us and we trust them. But when others push in and say hurtful things it is so difficult to concentrate on performing the Bhagotam for the sabbanda."

Saraiah butted in: "Mother Ellamma has explained everything so clearly, why do you keep questioning her?"

Ellamma admonished him: "No. You must understand. There is a special way in which girls are insulted or looked at, and it is very painful. She has been hurt and she's speaking about it. Let her talk. You're overreacting." Turning to Cina

Ellamma, she said, "Look, my girl! In this world, there are different kinds of people. Some walk all over us. Others depend on us to learn about their origins, the history of their community and what the future has in store for them. We've to work harmoniously with these different types of people and live among them. The best way for us is to attract them with our performance, to make it so riveting that they sit and watch for hours. That is the most fitting reply to those who try to ride rough over us."

She continued: "That's why you should focus on the advice Jambavathatha just gave you. Don't let yourself get hurt just because someone said something. Try not to let it worry you, and don't brood over it. That's why, at the beginning of each Bhagotam performance, we find it important to remind our audience: 'Brothers and sisters! We haven't come here just to make a living. We are here to tell you your history. You are our patrons. Give us good clothes, offer us paddy. But above all, do not treat us with indifference. Do not look down upon us.'"

Cendravva was also listening attentively to the discussion. Breaking the seriousness of the moment, Ellamma put her tongue out and twisted it sideways, asking: "Cendravva, has my mouth reddened?"

"Yes, very much so, Ellavva."

"What about yours, Cina Ellamma?" The girl put out her tongue. "As red as a parrot's!" she said affectionately and gave her a hug.

Cendravva quickly brought out a mirror and said, "Take a look." Everyone inspected their mouths, tongues and lips from all angles until they were satisfied.

Ellamma began again. She told them about her childhood. Addressing Cina Ellamma, who was still looking at the mirror, she said, "Listen, Cina Ellamma, do you know what happened one day? It was during the Razakars' time. I was twenty-one or twenty-two. Those were hard times. The dora folk used to be extremely cruel. The government was also oppressive. When I performed, people used to throw bundles of currency notes at me. Then when I bent down to pick them up, they would throw more on my back. Our children, who were hiding behind, used to collect the money. Some people would pin together currency notes into garlands and put them around my neck. This is just the advance, they would say, leering."

"Weren't you angered when they behaved like that? In our troupe, if anyone behaves badly you are so harsh with them." Cina Ellamma said.

"Wait ... you've heard only a part of the story. Looking at me, those high-caste young men used to say: 'You slut!'" I would reply, 'Sir, think of me as your younger sister.' Sometimes they would comment: 'She's getting too haughty and cunning.' I used to reply, 'It's only with your blessings that I'm so sharp and active.' I spoke that way trying to somehow grapple with the insults and the hurt, but actually I would be cursing them in my mind.

"When I couldn't bear it any longer I would say: 'Sir, I'm not a jogini or a jannah, an erpula or a yesa. I'm a Bhagotam performer and my task is to tell you the legends and the history of the sabbanda labouring–singing communities. Remember, I'm a married woman. I take care of you by teaching you your history and culture. I also take care of my parents. My husband came to my home to live with me. Don't treat me like a jogini. Please, I beg of you.'"

Unable to restrain herself, Cina Ellamma interjected: "But the jogini and other women you mentioned are our own people, aren't they?"

"Yes, they too are our people. But the brahman persecuted the Jambava muni and the madiga. The brahman are aryans and come from outside. They took away the land from the madiga who tilled the land and provided livelihoods for the sabbanda. The brahman decreed that the madiga must make shoes from the skins of dead animals and that they should do that work forever. They turned our women into jogini. They offered them to god. They turned them into yesa women. This was done to destroy madiga families and dynasties, to keep them away from power.

"Now, you may want to ask about our own men. Well, if any of them looked me up and down, I just used to give him a slap. I treated them as I would my fathers, brothers and sons. All the same, I could not but reprimand some men. I used to take the opportunity of doing this when I played Chenchulakshmi and Balanagamma. On stage I'd bring out all the anger and suffering hidden in my heart. I'd indirectly abuse some of the men sitting in the audience as if I was referring to Mayala Fakir or Srihari.[1] I'd stop only when they shrunk back in shame. Initially they were very angry, but gradually they changed, and grew more polite.

"The audience was usually awestruck when I played the lead role wearing many-coloured shells and a basket-load of jewellery. When I played the male and female roles with equal ease, they marvelled even more. All my life I have played Mother Ellamma; all my life I have sustained this art and, in turn, this art has sustained me.

"I could sing the most difficult tunes with ease. When I sang the bhupala ragam, my veins would stand out; the earth

1. Mayala Fakir is the villain who kidnaps Balanagamma in the mythological story *Balanagamma Katha*.

under my feet would vibrate. So also with the rupaka talam and adi talam. Impressed by my performance, Nataraju Ramakrishna and Amitabh Bachchan honoured me with the title 'Saraswati' and gave me the 'Hamsa' award. Saraswati did not bring me good luck! I fell sick with flu and was bed-ridden for many days. That's why I am Ellamma again."

We cannot tell whether Cina Ellamma and Saraiah understood everything or not, but their eyes grew large and they looked overwhelmed.

"But what about our story, the story of the chindu?" asked Saraiah.

Ellamma said, "For the sake of the labouring–singing people, we've cherished and upheld grandfather Jambava's heritage. We do not consider the brahman as superior to us. That is why in the Jambavapuranam the brahman are criticized so much."

"How did the reddy and velama behave?" asked Saraiah.

"They generally follow the brahman, behaving as though they were their tails! They would address us rudely as Elli, Saayiga, Kishti—their heads filled with arrogance. That is why they come to watch our Bhagotam reluctantly. But remember, traditionally when we performed the Bhagotam, the dora folk used to come and sit in chairs facing us, and get themselves abused by us. They would make us call them 'uncivilized people', 'sons of dogs', 'urine-drinkers' and so on because they believed that it would bring them good luck. But they didn't allow their women and children to watch our Bhagotam. It is said that they live in a world of arrogance. That's why the saying goes: if the velama lives in a village it will get ruined, just as a hut built outside the village gets ruined.

"Labouring–singing people start work before dawn and when they return home in the evening, the day begins for the reddy. He wakes up at that time. These communities don't do any work, but live like parasites and exercise power. "Whatever it may be, the Chindu Bhagotam has given us—you and me—life. By continuing grandfather Jambava's legacy, we have become the breath of the labouring–singing people. In turn, the sabbanda are our very breath. That's all."

Ellamma finished her story. Cina Ellamma's and Saraiah's eyes shone. Their faces grew bright like the sun emerging from dark clouds.

The three of them bade goodbye to the madiga elder and his wife Cendravva.

A few days later the troupe took leave from the sabbanda people of the village and set out to the neighbouring village to begin a new round of negotiations and performances.

TRANSLATED BY N. MANOHAR REDDY

TATAKI WINS AGAIN

Tataki

Spade on shoulder, Balamma patrolled the mud banks of the canal that bordered the groundnut fields. The stream wound its way around a rocky patch, bringing water to Balamma's land. She had just cut open the bund to let the canal water in. The mud walls around the other fields had not yet been cut, so the water flowed plentifully into her field. The groundnut beds filled rapidly. Balamma, who filled such large plots with water, was not yet twelve.

The karnam's bonded labourer had woken early and walked to the adjoining field in a hurry. By then, all but two of Balamma's plots had filled with water.

He swore at her. "When did you come in the dark like a ghost? Watered all your plots, eh? Water the last two later, I'm diverting the water to my field." He lowered his spade to block the stream flowing into her field with mud. That was it! The girl sped like a rocket and stomped down the mud bank he had just built.

"Move, old man!" She elbowed him and he fell onto the bund. "I have two more plots to water, they'll fill in no time," she said, as she returned to her field. "Don't you dare come near till then. You can divert the flow after I'm done."

The labourer stayed put, watching her and muttering curses. "This girl will not let a person move a hand or foot. How'll she look after her husband and family, tomboy that she is!" He lit a bidi and sat on the bund gloomily.

The last two plots filled up and Balamma's watering was done. She came up to the stream, washed the mud off her feet, and shouted "Grandpa! Dam the stream now. Divert the water to the karnam's field."

"You're a very kind girl! You just pushed me down on the bank, and now you are calling me grandpa," he said, getting up and redirecting the water. The water flowed into the karnam's first plot. It had not yet filled when the flow dropped to half. Cursing, he looked up. By then, the workers in the fields on both banks upstream had begun to draw water. The level in the canal had dropped completely.

"Oh god, this is the end of me! I rushed here in the morning chill but this chit of a girl came even earlier. Now, the others are here as well, letting water into their fields. How will these plots fill with such a thin flow? What if the karnam comes?" He sat cowering.

After washing her feet, Balamma untied the knot that held her skirt over her knees. She dusted it down, went to the neem tree on the main bank of her field and plucked a twig. She cleaned her teeth with the twig and looked out for her friends. Some of them had already brought their cattle to graze on the green thunga grass by the stream. Others were walking along the bund on the village tank. She considered who it might be fun to play gilli-danda with, and who would be good for a game of toss-the-pebbles. Her friend Marnagi had not yet arrived. But Narsadu and Yelladu, who played gilli-danda, were already there. She thought gleefully, 'Yesterday I hit the gilli so far, I had you both running like hell to catch it—come, I'll make you run again!' She quickly washed her face, ate some groundnuts fresh from the fields, and drank water. Then she ran to meet her friends.

"Have you brought your lunch bundles or will you go home?" she asked the boys.

"We have our lunch."

"Shall we play gilli-danda?"

"Yesterday I fell down while we were playing and scraped my knees. You both play," said Yelladu.

"Let me see," said Balamma. "The wound is dirty. Let's clean it and put jerri potha juice on it. But first go wash your leg in the lake."

Yelladu washed his legs and returned. In the marshland at the edge of the lake, the jerri potha grew lush. They plucked leaves off a tender bush and yellow milk flowed thick. Balamma applied it on Yelladu's leg with her finger and made him put some on his cracked lips as well. They both went back to Narsadu.

"How is the pain in your knee?" he asked.

"It has gone down a bit," said Yelladu.

"Okay. Stand on this side. Stop the gilli from flying into the lake. I'll stand on the other side and be the catcher," Narsadu said.

Taking the gilli and danda from where they had hidden it in a bush, Balamma hitched her skirt up over her knees. She drew a thick line on the ground and took aim, poised to strike the gilli on the line. She struck the ground near the gilli a few times and when she was ready, gave the tapered edge of the gilli a sharp tap, spinning it into the air and hitting it mid-flight. It didn't go too far the first time. Narsadu couldn't catch it either. He picked up the gilli and gave it back to Balamma. She took position again and hit it hard the second time. Now it went spinning in the air across the field, falling in a bush. A rabbit scampered out of the shrub and ran into the open. Yelladu saw it first.

"A rabbit! A rabbit!" he shouted. Balamma threw down the danda. They all picked up their sticks and ran after the animal. To its bad luck, it ran towards the edge of the lake. "Make it run into the lake. Don't let it run any other way," Balamma shouted. They cornered the rabbit, yelling loudly to confuse it "Ho, Ho, Ho, laba laba laba..." In that shouting, Yelladu started to sing:

Anantagiri Sami wants to play
Where has this rabbit gone away?

The rabbit, which had started running to the rocks, turned back towards the groundnut field. There Balamma, waving her stick, sang out:

Anantagiri Sami wants to play
The rabbit has come here to stay.

Wherever the rabbit ran, they blocked its path, shouting and singing. It finally ran towards the lake, jumped into the water and tried to escape.

"The rabbit is done for," said Balamma.

Yelladu disagreed. "It will swim away to the other bank."

"You think it will live long enough to cross the lake?!"

"What use is it to us if it dies?" asked Narsadu. "If it dies in the lake, the fish will eat it."

"Stupid! Why should we wait for it to cross the lake or to die in the middle? One of us must swim out and get it," said Balamma.

"Will you go, Yella?" asked Narsadu.

"No, I can't swim with my injured leg," replied Yelladu.

"Abbo! I won't go. The lake is so deep in the middle. I'm sure to lose my breath if I try to swim across it," protested Narsadu.

'These fellows are no good!' thought Balamma, tucking up her skirt between her legs and jumping into the lake. She swam purposefully in the rabbit's direction. Moving with the ease of a fish, she reached the rabbit in no time. She caught it by the scruff of the neck with one hand, and swam back to the bank. There, the other two took the rabbit from her and wiped it dry with their shoulder-towels.

Balamma took the animal home. Her father, Basayya, had heard about the rabbit on his way back from the bazaar. He turned on his heels, went to the toddy shop and bought a bottle. Just as Balamma reached home with the rabbit, her father walked in with the bottle of toddy. Balamma's mother Ananthamma looked at father and daughter in amazement. "Did you see your daughter bring in the rabbit in a dream? How else could you imagine getting the toddy? I didn't even know that she had caught a rabbit, how on earth did you find out? Anyway, father and daughter are a perfect pair," she teased.

"I am tired of eating tamarind curry and lentils everyday. You cook a tasty rabbit curry today and we can all enjoy ourselves," said Basayya.

★

The karnam's bonded labourer stood in the field, letting the plots absorb water from the meager flow into the canal. Just as he had feared, the landlord appeared.

The labourer's heart skipped a beat when he saw the landlord. Walking into the field, the karnam asked, "What is this? Why are you still here? Didn't you come here before dawn? The fields are not even half-filled with water!"

"I did come very early, dora," the labourer stuttered.

"Then who was here before you?" demanded the landlord, as he stood on the bund and saw the canal-bed downstream wet with water.

"How did that canal bed get wet? Basadu is in the village. How did his field get watered?" he asked, taking in the situation. His man was silent.

"So! His daughter is the one who filled those plots with water, isn't it? Yes, that Tataki! Wait, I'll straighten her out," muttered the landlord.

The labourer began to look very worried.

★

Ananthamma woke up by three-thirty, before the morning star rose in the sky. She cooked a meal and then swept the yard briskly with a broom made of the branches of the pulivayili tree. Hearing the sound, Basayya rose from his slumber. "Has Sangadu come?" he asked. With sleepy eyes, he broke a twig from the neem tree in front of the house to clean his teeth. He also broke a twig each for his children. Sangappa came into the yard, shouting "Basanno!"

"People are on their way to work and you are still cleaning your teeth!"

"There's nothing else that I have to do. I'll clean my teeth as I walk with you. I can wash my mouth and face at the Gaajupuram stream on the way."

Basayya picked up the lunch bundle kept ready by Ananthamma and wrapped it in his work towel. A large group of fellow-workers were already on their way, absorbed in different conversations.

"Anna, the festival is approaching. Have you bought clothes for your children?" asked Sangappa.

"When was it our lot to think of new clothes? I don't even have enough provisions in my house. We finished our meager store of food when we weeded our plots over these past ten days. The children are forever eating, like hens. We now have to buy sixteen seers of maize and twenty seers of rice. Whether they wear new clothes or not, my children should not have to worry about what they are going to eat. All my planning is only for this. I've already worked for four days. A few more days' work should bring in the money. My wife's wages will add to this amount. Balamma too has been of great help in watering the fields. Had she not done so, I would not have been able to come to work with you." As they walked, they came up to the stream and washed their faces.

★

"Why didn't you wake me up when Appa left?" Balamma chided her mother. "All our neighbours would have started watering their fields by now. There won't be enough for us."

"No one has gone to the fields yet, child. They haven't even woken up. Don't worry. It is still dark. Go when there is some more light," said Ananthamma.

"Ammo! The fields have to be watered now," said Balamma as she put on her slippers on her way out. She hurried through the chill wrapping herself with her towel. No one else was on the path. Some people were still sweeping their yards. Others were walking out to fetch water with their pots. Roosters had just begun to crow. "Wake up. You have to drive out the cattle," she heard mothers pleading with children pledged as bonded labour to some landlord or the other.

Listening to all these sounds, Balamma crossed the Kantha stream that split the mala and madiga settlements from the main village, and walked along the cart tracks between tall trees. It was not yet light and she could see no one around.

"Ammo! It is so dark. Wish I'd listened to my mother! Even so, what have I to fear? Everyone says I am a brave girl. I will not be afraid. Nobody can frighten me! But what if demons come? Anyway, I'll cross these tracks quickly and get to the other side in no time. By then it will be light," she said to herself as she broke into a run.

She reached the field and broke open the earth dam upstream with her spade. Water gushed into her field. The groundnut plots filled rapidly.

★

In the past, Basayya's grandfather, Veerayya, had been a bonded labourer to the karnam. After that his father Cendraiah too had been pledged. Later, when the landlords joined the Bhoodan movement, the present karnam's grandfather, Venkat Rao, decided to give his land to Veerayya in order to keep it safe. 'Can a bonded worker ever do agriculture on his own? Or will he just grow grass? He has no bullocks to plough and no tools to work with. Even if he had all these, he would never have the guts to till the land. Even if I donate the land to him today, I can take it back whenever I want. The land will be safe even through the Bhoodan movement,' he thought and parted with the land to earn a name for himself.

Just that year, the Land Ceiling Act came into force and to his misfortune, the landlord lost complete hold over that land. The government acquired the land given to Veerayya and gave it to him with a formal title. After Veerayya, Cendraiah inherited and tilled that land. Now Basayya owned it. Venkat Rao had told this story to his son, Narayan Rao, who in turn narrated it to his son, Tirumala Rao. All three generations had tried their best to snatch the land one way or another. And all three generations of the once-bonded family had somehow protected it from the landlords' hands. In this battle, their heads had been battered, their legs had been broken, and they had been assaulted time and again for no rhyme or reason. When all this had failed, the landlords had tried to buy the land cheaply. But even that didn't succeed.

The current karnam, Tirumala Rao, sat mulling over all this.

"Why do you look so troubled?" asked his wife, Alavelu Manga. Tirumala Rao glared at her. She hurried back indoors.

He was soon lost in his thoughts again. All his energy was focused on preventing Basayya from ever coming back to the field. 'Basadu shouldn't even enter the land. What can be done to ensure this? If he is killed, the matter will become public. He shouldn't be killed, but should be forced to leave the field and the village. What can be done to make this happen?' he thought.

He stood up abruptly from the chair as if struck by an idea, and walked out of the house.

"Go and guard the guava plantation near the big well," he ordered his bonded worker. "No need to water the ground-nuts today."

"Alright, master," answered the worker.

★

Balamma ate the food her mother had packed. She watered the plots at her leisure. The water couldn't reach places where the ground was high. She levelled those areas with her spade. 'Today, I must finish watering the plots,' she thought. She didn't play with her friends, nor did she sit even for a moment. Work, work, work—Balamma was simply lost in the work.

"My Balamma's nature is to work," her father often said proudly. "My father was like that too. When he died, his soul came into Balamma." When her father praised her this way, Balamma felt on top of the world. 'The watering should be completed before the sun sets; only then will I go home. My father will commend me,' she thought as she worked on.

The field next to Balamma's had a jowar crop so healthy it looked like sugarcane. Even tall men standing in the field could not be seen. There! Right from that field, the landlord sprang out, grabbed Balamma's hand and dragged her back. At first, she did not understand who was pulling her and why. After she saw his face, she recognized the karnam of the neighbouring groundnut field and felt a rush of fear. The karnam were of a higher caste. They would never touch a madiga. Why was he pulling her? It baffled her.

"Tataki! You bloody witch! You are a small girl, are you? What makes you come here like a man and water the groundnut fields? In our houses, girls like you don't step into the field. You mala and madiga don't even know that girls have to be kept at home! You are a small girl, are you?" Cursing her, he thrust his hand into her blouse. Her small hands couldn't throw off the landlord's fat paws. His body felt like an iron post. Balamma trembled all over. Her mouth went dry. One corner of her mind recalled the women in the mala and madiga settlements whispering about how the landlord had taken one woman or another.

Then it struck her. "This bastard is going to do something awful!" But she simply couldn't free herself from the landlord's hands. Not knowing what to do, she threw herself on to the ground. But he continued to drag her.

"Do I have to drag you now? Why should I waste my energy? Stand up and walk! Do you think I'll let you go if you fall on the ground?" he said, "I'll drag you like a fallen branch if I have to."

"Master! Let me go! I fall at your feet. Appo! Awwo! Ammo!" Balamma howled.

"Do you think they'll come running as soon as you call out? Will they stay alive if they do? Why are you shouting at the top of your voice?" thundered the karnam. "You really have a swollen head. You water the fields before my men, do you?" He slapped her hard on her cheek. Balamma was thrown to a distance. He went after her, grabbed her hand and bent over to drag her again. She took aim and kicked him as hard as she could on the groin with both her legs. "Oh! I am dead!" he said and fell back. She took her chance, raised herself and ran without looking back. "Tataki, you tramp! That demon is running away—catch her, catch her!" shouted the landlord as he collapsed.

In the village the mala and madiga women giggled through their sari ends as they shared the news, "The landlord wanted to catch our Balamani. She kicked him in the groin!"

TRANSLATED BY R. SRIVATSAN

THE VILLAGE TANK'S LAMENT

Oorajeruvu Kadupu Kota

Why do you stare at me like that, open-mouthed? Don't you remember? You used to walk along this bund with your mother when you were a little child. You have come with your father too. When your brother herded the buffaloes along the embankment, you tagged along, cradling a buffalo calf. Carrying a basket of groundnuts, you walked alongside your mother when she took your father his lunch bundle of rotte. If your grandmother went to the fields with her winnowing pan, broom and kunchi to glean the paddy that had been left behind on the ground, you would throw a tantrum saying that you wanted to go along, and follow her all along my embankment. To dissuade you she would linger, pull out some betel leaves from the bag tucked into her waist and sit here, chewing them. She would give you a small one too. You would chew it up as fast as you could, and then stick out your piquant tongue to check how red it had become. You were so thrilled to go with your grandmother!

"My child, this is not easy work. You have to search out the grain wherever it lies, sweep up the gleanings and carry them back. Your feet are tiny and still tender. They'll bruise and ache. Stay back. If you cry like this now, there'll be no paddy left for us to glean. Listen to me, my darling," she would plead and send you back. If that did not work, she would say, "If you do as I say, I promise to get you a nose-ring with a red stone." That would always calm you down.

When you returned from school, you and your brother would walk in a single file on the embankment and go to your mother in the fields—can you recall at least that now?

My girl! Don't tell me I have changed so much that you do not know me. I was once spread over thirty acres, and now I have been confined to these thirty square yards. Is there no way I can save myself? Earlier, however heavy the rains, there would be no floods. As the waters rose, they would pour into me. I would swell like a putti-measure brimming with paddy.

I lay close to the village and shined like the moon. On full moon nights, I competed with her as I glittered. During the rains, when I was full of water, the acres of black soil on my banks would be layered with silt. A thick growth of dark green thunga, aapu and tubers would spread over the silt. Leafy greens like gangavaila koora and gongura sprouted up here and there. On the way home after weeding the fields, women would pick the leaves of these edible greens and bundle them into their saris. With the bundles tucked into their waists they all looked pregnant, and the older women looked really comic.

Come summer, the adults would swim in the wells around the village, but the small children would come here to learn. When they felt confident enough, they too would leave for the wells. There was always plenty of water for the cattle—and not just of this village. Let me share something else with you, my granddaughter: children who graze the cattle and field labourers reach home at dusk. Between twilight and the night, there is still some light, is there not? At that time, deer with huge horns, sarangis, cheetahs, foxes, wolves, wild dogs and peacocks would come from the forests in the east, drink their fill and return. The rabbits came in swarms from the hillocks of the north, and from the fields down south.

When the rains were heavy, I would fill up and flow over the embankment. Once the rain cascaded down for two days without pause. Water gushed into me from all kinds of places. I feared that I would get so full that the embankment would burst. Waves lashed against my sides as if I was raising the alarm. The neeretollu rushed to the embankment and called to those living beneath it to leave their houses. They watched with bated breath as the neeretollu opened the valves of the tank and the water flowed out. It flooded the houses below the tank. If the neeretollu had not arrived at that exact moment, the embankment would surely have burst. What was it that made them come? Who had told them? These questions were uppermost on everyone's minds. The water level fell. Overcome with gratitude, everyone spoke to the neeretollu affectionately addressing them as if they were family—as kaka, mama, bava.

The neeretollu said: "Ayya, we were peacefully asleep. Around midnight, we heard cries, 'Orey Mallaiah, Orey Cendraiah, the embankment is giving way!' We jumped up and ran here. When we arrived, the embankment was already at breaking point. The waves dashed against the sides of the tank, making a thunderous sound. That is why we called out to the people below and opened the valves immediately."

Who could it have been other than Katta Mysamma who had roused them? The village will have a festival this year in her honour, the neeretollu vowed. With the rains so heavy and the tank filling up, the old water in the tank flowed out, and new water came in; the canals outside the village grew full.

There were schools of fish at the sluice gates. They had hidden thus long in my womb. Now they swam out happily, along with the water, with their mouths open, twirling their moustaches. Did the villagers not catch these fish and enjoy eating them? I don't know whether you will believe me, but when I saw the people who had eaten fish, I felt really happy. Of course, I was also sad about the fish. You have heard so many stories now—can you recall even one of them?

In the summer, the water level receded and huge rocks surfaced. Women would thrash their washing against them. One day, a woman came with her baby. She left the baby playing high up, far from the water, and busied herself with the washing. The child wandered down to the water and sneaked into the sluice pipe. He sat there playing right in the middle. When the mother looked for the baby, she could not find him. Then she peeped into the sluice. There he was, happily sitting inside the pipe. However much she called him and entreated him, he would not budge. Other women came and tried to cajole him. The mother was desperate: she wailed, beating her hands against her head and against her chest. But the boy stayed put. Truth be told, even I got worried. Then one of the women had an idea. She walked back to the village and returned with another child whom she seated on the bank opposite the sluice. She called out to the baby inside, "Look, look. Look at this child!" The other child laughed and played: he beat at the water in excitement. Saying "Ha ha ha-chi", the infant inside the sluice came toddling out. His mother ran to pick him up and held him close.

All this took place a long time ago. But mothers still tell that story. Those who bring their toddlers near me now make sure to look after them very carefully.

There is another story about me. Do you know it? A madiga was walking his he-buffalo along my embankment. God knows what went through the he-buffalo's mind. It stopped suddenly, and dug in its heels. It wouldn't go forward, it wouldn't move backward, it just stood there motionless. The madiga waited, wondering what had happened to the animal. The animal had seen the tank on one side of the embankment looking like a pot filled to the brim. On the other side he saw the unploughed fields. 'Vayammo, vathandro! Oh my mother! Oh my father! I have to plough all these fields!? This tank is full of water and all this land is ready to be ploughed—and all by me! I will die before all this work is completed. Oh God!'— the he-buffalo thought, took fright, broke his heart, and died. Those who labour tell this tale to people who take fright when they hear about the work that is to be done.

Are you looking for the channel below the sluice, the Katta Mysamma shrine and the doughty tamarind tree behind it? You are of an age now when you know the difference between happiness and sorrow. Look carefully, you will find all these, but they have changed. At that time, women would bathe near the big sluice gate and men near the small one. They would also wash their clothes there. Often women would say, 'However much dirt we wash out, Gangamma will hide it in her womb like a mother.'

After the water receded, people would load donkeys with lumps of the black silt and carry it away. One would think that potters had magic in their hands when they fired pots for the village and piled these as high as hills. When the panipatalollu came to me to fulfil their vows—the baindla would bring their pots, big and small, for the jeldi festival the eedigollu would come to dedicate their toddy pots, and the madiga to worship

Ellamma, their pots daubed with turmeric and kumkum, decorated with shells and neem branches—I felt as a mother does when her children return to her home.

Farmers, small and big, would transport the silt in bullock carts and spread it on the fields readied for paddy. The black silt would nourish the soil, and I would have more space to fill up with water. Branches of the ganuga tree were ploughed into the soil. These nourished the earth and increased the yield. At that time, who had heard of fertilizers like urea? Agricultural workers of the village—mala, madiga, kummari, kammari, chakali, mangali, golla, kuruma, eediga, salé, mudiraju—all of them, both men and women, de-silted me. I remember all this well. Pregnant women and aged people carried mud. Children too carried mud to the embankment in small baskets, playing and singing all the while. No one thinks of me anymore. If the lands below me have to get sufficient water, do I not have to fill up? If I have to fill up, do I not have to be deepened? If I have to be deepened, the silt needs to be removed, doesn't it? This is an age-old system.

The sabbanda used to come together and de-silt me once in five or ten years. After the yaski and rabi crops, people would take the yield home. During summer, when there was no work in the fields they would rest or work at home. To increase the yield, they would call the chindollu to perform the Bhagotam. On the first day, when they performed the Jambava Puranam, the goddess Ellamma herself would come to me and propitiate me. A neerati would come, prostrate before Ellamma, and wash her face with my water. Ellamma would then climb the embankment. At that time, everyone would come to take a dip in the water. They would ululate, crying 'poligoliga' and responding 'salaam poligalugani' to propitiate me. The whole village would reverberate with the sounds. You know about goddess Batukamma—villagers would bring the Batukamma and let it float into my lap. How happy, how beautiful I would feel! I cannot put it in words.

If you want to know whose lands lie below the tank and are watered by me—well, they belong to the dora and the rich farmers. Such people always think that sacks of paddy and wads of notes should come easily, but they don't spare a thought for the land or for me. Those who care for me don't have lands below me. If they do have lands, these are not irrigated by the tank. They can only cultivate their lands when it rains. At other times they have to work as wage labour in the big fields. They are vetti people, aren't they? They can live only if they work. They belong to the sabbanda castes. They are also the people who de-silt me.

One day, Madiga Ellamma, walking on the embankment, called out, "How great you were in earlier times! What has become of you now? You helped us survive even during the droughts. You saved small children and the aged during the great famine. During the hottest of summers, villagers roamed around you like ants. We would collect lapfuls of roots and tubers. We roasted some at night and boiled the rest. Everyone ate them. We survived the famine because of you. But going by what is happening now, in the future we may not even be able to get the fruit or the leaves of the hardy balusaku.

"It took such a long time before the mala-madiga could become sarpanch, the headman. But meanwhile the earth beneath our feet vanishes. In front of us, you and the greenery around you are both vanishing. But who notices? Is there anyone who will do something about it? If there is someone, only god knows where they are working and what they are doing. We work for everyone, but no one works for us. Look at your plight—you, who helped us survive," she said.

I hoped that they would de-silt me. But by the time Madiga Yerra Balappa became sarpanch, everything had changed. The sarpanch lost powers over the repair of tanks and ponds. Not just this, there was little else left in his power. What could he do? Water-user associations sprang up. I have no idea what water they work for. They don't care for me. What can I say, my grandchild? My soul is like molten sand. You can say anything you want. I'll tell you something—only don't tell this to anyone. No one will look after me except the labouring castes. Only they need me. The world will run only if our relationship is maintained. The others are after easy money, easy gold. They want to grow rich doing no work and are damaging me. They dig bore-wells, cutting into my womb. If these are to have water, don't they know that I must fill up?

The other day Madiga Ellamma called out, "All around us we find shameless greed. We are caught in the middle. People have become false. We are of no use."

You speak the truth, Ellamma my daughter. Let your stomach grow full with porridge. What other option do I have? I must wait for the time of the labouring–singing castes.

TRANSLATED BY GITA RAMASWAMY

OBSTACLE RACE

Gandalu

The overflowing stream wound itself around the village like a snake winds itself around a man. Hedging the banks of the stream were mango trees. The mangoes had very interesting names. Corn Mango, the insides of which looked like corn pearls; Juicy Mango; Round Mango; Coconut Mango; Blue Mango; Spicy Mango; Goat's Udder Mango, because they always came in pairs like the goat's udder; Crooked Mango and so on. The Spicy Mango is extremely sour and tangy when raw, but when it is ripe it is sweeter than words can tell.

All the trees were now bare. They should actually have been in full bloom but they were all leased to the Tandur folks, who came, plucked all the fruit and took them away. Those that remained were on the farthest branches hidden away by the leaves.

A gang of children was searching frantically for these remaining mangoes. Adivi was leading them from the front. His full name was Adivaiah. His mother gave birth to him when she went weeding the green-gram fields. Since he was born in the forest, adivi, he was called Adivaiah. He was carrying a long stick made from the vayili tree branch. The stick was taller than him and he used it to move the branches and thick foliage that densely covered the paths. He moved bent low as he made his way through it all. The others followed his lead.

It seemed as if the mango season was coming to an end no sooner than it had started. The children spent the entire time up on the trees. At the crack of dawn, as soon as he had rinsed his mouth with water, Adivi would disappear from his home and reappear on their high branches.

That day, while he was searching for the leftover fruit, the patel reddy boy and Madiga Narasimha stood underneath keeping watch. Adivaiah was plucking the fruits and throwing them down. He had chosen a nice, tasty fruit on the tree and eaten it.

As he reached out for another mango, the branch beneath his feet gave way, as did the one he was holding on to. He slipped and fell, hitting against several branches on his way down. The ground was covered with thorny shrubs of the mogali flower and rows of hemp. He slid along these and finally landed in the stream. He was dazed and hurt. Adivi's friends raced to the spot and crowded around him.

"Orey Adivi! Please get up, get up! You'll drown in these waves ... get up!" they shouted and started crying.

But Adivi did not move. He just lay there unconscious and still. His frightened friends felt helpless and started wailing even more. Crying, they dragged him to the shore. They examined his legs and hands closely to see if he was hurt. They held his chin and shook his face to wake him up. Adivi opened his eyes and rose to his feet slowly. His whole body was aching. "Amma!" he groaned. His head was bleeding. His mouth was dry. His friends helped him sit up and brought him water in leaf cups from a nearby freshwater ditch. They wiped the blood slowly and holding him carefully by the shoulders they took him back into the village.

Even as they were reaching the cattle-feed barn they heard a voice, "O Adivi!" That very instant, the friends holding Adivi dropped him and fled with great speed along different paths. They all knew that the voice belonged to Adivi's father. Even Adivi himself, who had been weak, scared and drained of all energy until then, gathered strength from god knows where to dive into the paddy stacks heaped on the left. He was afraid his father would scold him for climbing trees. As he hid in the stacks, his eyelids drooped again and he fell asleep hiding there.

Calling out "Adivi! O Adivi!" his father searched the entire village. Someone must have told him that his son had hurt himself and that he was now sleeping in the paddy stacks, so the father came to the stacks and began pleading with Adivi, "I won't beat you son. Come, let's go home." When he found him, he carried his son home. He wiped the boy's body with warm water, fed him some rotte and made him drink water. He spread out the mat and a sheet, and asked Adivi to lie down. Then he rubbed some fresh butter on the wounds.

"With Ellamma's blessings you managed the obstacle of the tree. That's one obstacle successfully overcome. But don't ever climb trees again or you'll hurt yourself like today," he said to his son as he sat beside him, gently patting his back to put him to sleep.

*

Usappa had been plying the cycle rickshaw on the same stony path for the last ten years. He was a father of five children and each day's earnings were never quite enough to feed the family for that day.

Usappa's mind was clouded with thoughts. 'I should buy new clothes for the children at least for the next Eronka festival. After all, it is a major event in the village—all the bulls are decorated, fed well and taken out in a procession. We should make something sweet that day. Or else the children will be looking longingly at everyone around.'

'We need to send the boy to school this year. He's growing older and it is time he started his studies. He doesn't sit still. Why! Even his grandfather was saying that Adivi is very intelligent. Now, with no schooling, all his intelligence seems focused on climbing trees. Grandpa is right. The boy is wasting his time. Yesterday he was lucky to survive that dangerous fall. It could have been so much worse.'

As he cycled, Usappa was mulling over how frightened his son must have been when he fell. Suddenly the rickshaw slowed down and began to drag. "Now what's wrong with this vehicle," he muttered as he got off to take a look. The rear left tyre was punctured. He looked around and went to Mechanic Karimsaab's shop nearby.

"Karimsaab," he pleaded, "I'll repay the old debt and pay you for this too, soon. My tyre is punctured, please fix it. You are a real friend."

"Arey Usappa!" Karim said, "You don't need to say all this. I know my money will be safe with you. Just leave the rickshaw here. I'll fix it no time. I don't have any other customers at the moment."

Soon Usappa's rickshaw was ready to go.

He asked a passer-by who was dressed in trousers and shirt, "What's the time?" When the man said it was noon, Usappa exclaimed, "Oh! It's time for me to go back to the village. I'm taking my boy to the schoolmaster to get him admitted into the school." Saying this, he hurriedly bid goodbye to Karimsaab and cycled home.

★

The village was lush green and beautiful with trees, streams and brooks. But it had no school building. They were running the school in the dargah, in the open space where the Muharram pirs were kept. All the reddy, brahman, sabbanda and Muslim children went to this school. From among the madiga, only Bangarigani Narasimha went to school. That year Manikkappa was the schoolteacher. Usappa would sometimes take the teacher in his cycle rickshaw to the nearby town, Kothapet.

One day, as Manikkappa Sir sat in the rickshaw, he said, "Usappa, your boy is really smart. Why don't you send him to school?" These words had remained stuck in Usappa's head.

As he pedalled furiously, he said to himself, "No matter what, the boy should be in school today. However long it takes or whatever happens!" Having made up his mind, he took Adivi to school and got him admission.

Adivi was thrilled with school!

He really liked the upma they gave during lunch-time. Some days it was wheat upma and on other days it was corn upma.

"It's really tasty!" he would brag to his playmates in the village.

But when they asked—"How do you eat it, Adivi? It's in the school, right? There are no vessels there for you to eat, are there?"—he would fall silent and say no more. Their conversation would end abruptly. But the upma was really filling! And by the time he went home to drink water and played around a bit, he had to be back at school. The teacher would be ready to start lessons and school would resume. After two hours, the schoolday would end with the loud ringing of the bell and everyone would go home.

Adivi was not only a much loved and petted son, but also a much-loved grandson. Whenever his grandfather went to town, he would say, "Adivi, do you want to come along?" He never let Adivi walk on the way; he would carry him on his shoulders. And as they walked, grandfather and grandson would chat.

"You are now going to school. What do you learn there, Adivi?" grandfather asked one day.

Adivi told him first about the upma and only later about the lessons. "Thatha, the upma is really tasty but … the peon, Bugappa Thatha, always gives us the upma in old newspaper sheets taken from the shelf outside. We eat the upma in paper while all the reddy, kapu, sabbanda and Muslim boys eat it in aluminium plates."

Whenever this matter came to his mind Adivi's face would grow sad. He became moody. "But all the same, I don't know why he gives us more upma than the rest of the boys," said Adivi, as he shared his worry.

Grandfather acted as if this whole thing did not really matter. Making light of the whole affair, he said, "Oh! That might be because he thinks our boys don't eat well at home … he thinks these boys are poor, let me give them more."

Grandfather's words soothed Adivi's troubled mind.

★

When the school closed for summer, all the other schoolchildren spent their time playing. But early every morning, Adivaiah went with his mother to pick up the dung at the dora's house. As his mother collected the dung into baskets, he carried them away and emptied them into the compost pit. Later he went with the other children of his neighbourhood to gather firewood. In the afternoon he took the calves out to graze.

After all this, whatever free time he got, he loved to spend it climbing trees. Adivi was most happy when he sat on the trees and ate the freshly plucked fruits. He would of course fill both his pockets to the brim with fruit for his friends before he climbed down.

On summer afternoons, soon after the half-day school got over, Adivi would throw his schoolbag at home and hurry to join the other children who were on their way to swim in the field well. While all of them swam in the well, Adivi would stay at the well's margins and slowly play around. One day the boys were climbing onto the bund around the well and diving into the well like they did every day. One boy teased Adivi. He said, "Why don't you go dive in along with the other boys? The water is not very deep."

Adivi thought to himself, 'That must be true—all the boys are able to dive in so easily!'

He waited until most of the boys had left and then climbed onto the bund and took a dive! Once he was in the water he realized it was more than he could handle—he gasped for breath as he bobbed in and out of the water, desperately trying to stay afloat. The other children were panic-stricken watching this. Madiga Mallanna, the patel's farmhand, happened to be nearby. He came running and jumped into the well to rescue Adivi. He caught him by his hair and dragged him out of the tank. He slapped the boy on the back to bring him out of shock. Then he took him home, handed him over to his parents and cautioned: "Don't ever come near the well until you've learnt to swim."

"Adivi! You could have drowned," said Usappa. "You managed to overcome yet another obstacle today."

The very next day he took his son to the patel's new well that lay to the north of the village. He took a sturdy rope along with him, tied it to Adivi's waist and lowered the boy into the water. He showed him how to move his hands and legs.

After a few days, when he was sure Adivi had picked up the technique, he set the boy to practice after tying the lightweight logs of the saga tree to his waist. Gradually Adivi's swimming improved. He began with small dives into the well and soon learnt to dive in with his legs crossed. He also learnt to hold his breath long enough underwater to dive in at one spot and re-emerge at another spot a distance away. He could even dive in to bring up the soft mud from the tank's bottom.

Adivi was now adept at all the swimming games the children played.

★

Not long after Adivi joined school, the schoolteacher was transferred to another village and his place was taken by a new teacher called Siddappa Sir. He belonged to the balija caste. Adivi had progressed from *Aa, Aaa* to *Lu, Luu* in the Telugu alphabet. The new teacher taught him *E, Ee, Aai* and *O, Oo, Ow* and Adivi mastered them in a single day. The teacher moved onto the set of consonants like *Ka, Kha*. He was very pleased with the speed with which Adivi picked up the alphabet.

He said to Adivi, "I'm very happy with your writing—I think you should move to a higher grade."

At first, Adivi felt very strange going to the high school. All the kapu, brahman, reddy and Muslim children sat on the benches; only Adivaiah and Madiga Narasimha sat on the floor. Two years passed by. The classrooms changed, but while all the other students sat on benches, these two continued to sit on the floor.

One day the Deputy Education Officer came to the third grade for inspection. He asked the students many questions. Most of the children were able to answer simple questions but couldn't tackle the more difficult ones. Adivi was the only one who could answer the difficult questions. This included questions about multiplication tables, and from a lesson, "The Letter", in their Telugu reader. Adivi even did additions and subtractions on the blackboard. The officer was all praise for him.

But when Adivi walked back from the blackboard to take his place on the floor at the end of the classroom, the officer noticed this. He told the teacher sternly, "Why did you make those boys sit on the floor? Let them sit on the benches along with all the others."

The teacher promptly moved Adivi and Narasimha from the floor on to the benches. After the inspection, Adivi acquired a new status in the eyes of the students and the teachers. They began to appreciate him better. Adivi now sat on a bench, equal with all the other children. There was no need to lift up his head to see the children sitting high on the benches—he only had to move his head sideways and he could see everyone.

The teacher even began to call upon Adivi to give the 'nose-and-cheek punishment' to all the children who had bunked classes and those who didn't finish their homework. Adivi had to hold their noses tight and slap their cheeks. He also had to make them stand on the benches as part of the punishment.

Varalakshmi, who was the teacher's daughter, Ramesh, Prabhakar and Raju were Adivi's best friends. But he had to 'punish' them too, if necessary. It was especially difficult to give Ramesh the nose-and-cheek punishment. Ramesh was popularly known as 'Snot-nosed Ramesh' and Adivi was worried that if he held Ramesh's nose, the snot would stick to his hand. Despite this when the time came, he would hold Ramesh's nose tight and slap his cheeks. As for the rest of the friends, they would plead with him: "Adivi please slap me lightly. I'll buy you a sweet rasgulla during the interval."

The rasgulla was tempting and they were his friends, so Adivi would oblige, and slap them lightly. Some children would however threaten him: "If you slap me hard or pinch my nose hard, just wait till interval time and see what I do to you!"

★

It was a history lesson on 'Social Reform Movements' that day. The teacher was explaining to the children what 'inter-caste marriages' were. In the course of the lesson he said, "An inter-caste marriage is one in which, for example, a savarna Hindu boy marries an untouchable girl. Or let's say Adivi in our class, who was born in a baindla caste, gets married to Madavi who belongs to the reddy caste."

No one knows how, but this statement reached Madavi's father's ears. The next day thirty to forty reddy confronted the teacher and began abusing him: "How dare you suggest a marriage between our girl and a baindla boy?"

They were all ready to beat up the teacher. The other teachers begged them to calm down and finally managed to send them away. The teacher had to go away on long leave from the very next day.

That year Adivi completed his third grade. He stood first in his class with more marks than the patel and sabbanda boys. He had to go to Tandur, the nearby town, to enrol in the fourth grade. The school was called Vijaya Vidyalayam. The centre of the school compound was full of mango, guava and neem trees and different flowering plants. There was only one entrance with a huge gate through which you entered the school. As soon as he stepped in, Usappa removed the handkerchief covering his head. He saw the watchman approaching and greeted him with a respectful bow. "Sir, I need to enrol this boy in the fourth standard."

The watchman gestured towards the office room on the right side. Usappa went into the office, showed them all the certificates he had brought along with him and got Adivi's name into the register.

The children who got less marks joined other schools by paying admission fees or through a recommendation from someone influential. It was strange to see all the kapu, reddy and tenugu children sat together on the very first day in the new school. In the village, they used to keep their distance from each other and mostly played with their own neighbours and caste group.

Adivi walked to Tandur every day to attend school. It was all very exciting—a new school! A higher grade!

All the children would bring lunch boxes to school. Since the Murshad Dargah nearby had drinking water, they would all sit there and have lunch. Adivaiah's tiffin box usually had punti-leaf curry and rice. The others usually had red lentils with rice and mango pickle. They would ask Adivaiah to sit at a distance from where they sat to eat. If they ever offered him their lunch they would carefully serve it without Adivi's hands touching their vessels. Adivi would be furious. He would curse them in his mind: "You sons of… It was okay to get the nose-and-cheek punishment from me in class, but you don't want to touch me here."

He made up his mind to get back at them somehow. He was waiting for the right time. One day it rained heavily and soon there was knee-deep water flowing everywhere. The path was covered with water and slush. Adivi pretended to slip and fall in the mud and slush on the path and caught hold of the other kids touching them in the process. Even the younger children always addressed him with the familiar 'Ra' and 'Orey'.

They would say, "Orey Adivi, why did you fall on me like this? My parents will scold me for touching you."

"What can I do? I slipped in the mud, I had no choice," Adivi would reply.

He was very pleased with himself. He realized that this was a good way to tease the other children. He would chase them and threaten to touch them. They would run here and there to avoid him, and would slip and fall in the mud! Adivi would laugh loudly and all the other children would join in. These were the games he played with his classmates.

★

That day the teacher was teaching poetry. He made the students repeat the metrical verse after him. Reciting the verses along with all his other classmates was a new and thrilling experience for Adivi. He wanted to listen to his own voice amidst the chorus of all the other voices. So he began to sing a bit more emphatically and loudly. The teacher was walking up and down the class with his hands behind him. He was observing the students to see which ones were singing loudly and well. When he noticed some children were not singing properly, he said: "Students, you should be loud and clear! Just look at Adivaiah—he's singing so well. Follow his lead!"

Adivi was immensely pleased to hear this praise from the teacher. With the exception of his parents and his grandfather, no one had ever praised him for anything in his village. His mother would praise when she needed him to fetch something from the grocery shop.

She'd say: "My son helps me a lot... If I say, Adivi run to the shop and fetch some salt, he runs there and is back in no time!"

His father would say: "If I say Adivi run to Saber's shop and fetch me an Azam beedi pack, he speeds away like a dragonfly."

His grandfather would say: "My grandson is so clever. He can make predictions of things to come better than the gods themselves."

But now to hear the teacher say that he was good at his studies—that too in the class, to all the students—made Adivi extremely happy.

In a flash he also remembered what the elder patel of his village had said to him about his studies. At that time Adivi's mother used to work in the patel's house. She used to clear the dung in the cow and buffalo shed. They would go early at dawn. She would say: "Son, come along with me and help me. I'll gather all the rubbish in baskets, please carry it to the rubbish pit."

The scene from that time was still fresh in his mind. That memory set him thinking and he forgot to recite the verse. The teacher noticed this and said, "Adivi, what happened to you? You were reciting the verses so well. Maybe I shouldn't have praised you."

Adivi gathered himself and began singing loud and clear again. But his mind was pulling him back to that incident.

★

Adi Venkatarami Reddy was teaching his eight-year-old son, Raji Reddy, to write the auspicious words 'Saraswati' and 'Om' on a slate. Adivaiah, who was also eight years old at that time, stood watching them, leaning on the long stick stuck under his chin with his leg crossed over it. Every evening, it was the same scene. Watching Adivi watching them irritated Venkatarami Reddy. Vexed, he asked one day, "O Adivi, why do you always stare at us with your big bulging eyes! Do you also want to learn to write?"

"Yes, Patel Sir," said Adivi.

The patel fetched a broken slate and a piece of chalk and wrote 'Saraswati' on the slate and asked Adivi to go sit on the stone bench outside and write over it again and again. Adivi sat where he was told and earnestly began writing.

Every evening at the same time, Adivi would come to the patel's house to tie up the calves in the shed and feed them. He would mind the calves while the older farmhand milked the cows and buffaloes. After the milking was done, Adivi would leave the calves free and sit down to his writing. He sat on the stone bench and learnt a new alphabet a day.

One day the oldest patel of the house, Rami Reddy—the child Raji Reddy's grandfather—saw Adivi at his studies. He found this very strange. He asked, "Who is teaching this fellow Adivi to read and write?"

"My father," his grandchild replied.

"Your father is a fool and you are one too. What a thing to do! Teaching that boy to read and write indeed. That fellow is a crafty rascal even without any education. He is a baindla boy. The baindla ... they are into all kinds of worship and even witchcraft. Imagine what they will do once they are educated. They're going to take over our temples. Give this fellow some education and he'll turn into a real sorcerer. So just stop this nonsense, you idiots. Stop it!"

Those words rang loud and burnt his ears. They filled his heart with an unknown fear and anxiety.

With a start Adivi came back to the present moment—he was in the classroom.

"The crafty rascal will turn into a real sorcerer!" Why did the patel say that?

Those words echoed in his mind again. Pondering over this, he joined the chorus of verse-singing in class once again.

The bell rang. It was time to go home. Grandfather had come to school after some shopping. Adivi walked home with him.

On the way he joyfully told his grandfather, "Grandpa, my teacher praised me before the entire class today."

"Really! What did you do, son?" asked his grandfather.

And Adivi began to narrate the events in the class. As he recounted them, he also told his grandfather about the incident at the patel's house and the words that the older patel had used —"Crafty rascal! Sorcerer!"

Grandpa said, "Adivi, you are amazing. You even remember things that happened last year. It seems as if you can hold the entire world in your head."

"There are many trials to be faced at every step. First get past all of these and then you can really become a sorcerer," he said, as he affectionately rubbed his grandson's back.

TRANSLATED BY UMA BHRUGABANDA

RAW WOUND

Radam

Father was at work in the ploughed field, levelling the ridges and removing weeds from the red soil. At home, mother searched anxiously for someone who could carry his lunch bundle to him. She was in a hurry to leave for her work site, and told her friend, Nagamma, "Let me know if anyone is going towards the red hillock where my husband is, I need to send him his meal."

A moment later, Nagamma shouted to my mother from behind the house, "My child, Ananthamma, no one I know is going in that direction. It is time, and the men will be looking homeward for their food. Take care of this matter, and then start for work as soon as you can."

Not knowing what to do, mother thought of abandoning her day's work, but hesitated, muttering: "For the last four days, fifteen of us have bent down and planted paddy without having stood erect for a moment. I'll get my wage of forty rupees today. But I'll lose the money if I don't go." She tied the bundle of rotte and lentils silently, and filled the aluminium pot with buttermilk. She put a small bit of charcoal in the white buttermilk to protect it from the evil gaze, and wondered who could carry it to Appa.

"I'll take it, you go on to work," I blurted, without even thinking. Mother's face was worth seeing—it shone with the brightness of five moons.

"Will you, my dear?" she exclaimed. She rushed into the kitchen, bringing a bit of soot and marked my foot, palm and temple to protect me from the demons on the way. "Be careful now. Walk on the side of the path, looking ahead—don't stumble on the stones. If any old men joke with you and ask you to look here or there, don't," she said.

I put the rotte bundle on my head and started walking. 'My father will be very pleased. He'll praise me,' I thought and wanting to meet him quickly, hastened along. As I crossed the road and entered the path between the fields, grandpa Talaari Samuel saw me. He was surprised. "What, my granddaughter! You are now old enough to carry food to your father, are you? Go carefully, little one," he said.

"Okay grandpa," I replied. After going some distance, I placed the buttermilk pot and the lunch bundle down on a black rock, turned my stiff neck this way and that, shook my numb arms and clenched my aching fists. I took a sip from the buttermilk and wiped my mouth. Putting the bundle back on my head, I picked up the pot and began walking again.

Uncle Anthaiah, bringing his cattle back from the grazing grounds, said to me, "Is it you, my niece, carrying your father's lunch? Look, an eagle is carrying a chicken up into the clouds —look up!"

"Uncle! I'll throw you over my shoulder," I retorted half-angrily. He was bluffing, and my mother had warned me about this. I didn't look up and hurried on. It was time to eat. Appa would be hungry, and looking towards the house. I walked faster. I finally reached the field. Appa had not yet stopped levelling—he kept working. He saw me and leapt on to the boundary and walked up to me. He took the bundle and the pot of buttermilk and put it down.

"My dear, you have brought the food at the right time, just when I was beginning to feel hungry," he said happily. He then growled, "Why have you brought the food? Your mother should have done so."

"Mother would have come, but today is the last day of her labour contract and they will pay her wages. I heard this and offered to bring the food. I also wanted to see the fields," I replied.

He beamed at me. "My smart girl, she has a large, courageous heart—just like my mother did." Both of us sat down to eat. When we were done, Appa said, "Sit under the tree, my child," and got back to work.

It was winter, when the sun sets in the evening like a diving bird. Appa hurried up, wanting to finish this plot to the boundary, so that he could start the next field tomorrow. I couldn't see him at work now. Just then, he called. "Syamamma, come here!" I ran to him, hoping to see him work from up close. "The levelling plank is not sinking into the earth properly—the weighing stone on it is not heavy enough. Be a good girl and sit on the plank," he said.

I agreed happily, pulled my skirt up between my legs, cross-tied my braids and sat on the levelling plank. Up close, I could see the plank digging into the ridges between the furrows clearly, as my weight pushed it down. It lifted the soft moist mud underneath, which frothed over in its sweet scent. I saw without sadness the weeds being pulled out with their roots. 'It is, after all, to plant crop that the weeds are removed,' I remembered.

Just then, my father said, "Don't look down, you'll get mud in your eyes!" My thoughts interrupted, I raised my eyes and looked ahead. In a while, the soil became softer. "That's it. You can get off now. Go sit under the morinda tree," my father said. I did as told.

The breeze wafted lovely smells from different sides. From the field to the left, the mature tuvar dal branches, deep green and filled with flowers, gave off their fresh aroma. From the right, the growing jowar field with its lush leaves rustling in the wind, sent its new green scent. I went amid the jowar plants. The leaves, running sap, beckoned me. It was different in each place: on some leaves, they were like sweet sugar-like crystals, on others, they glistened in the sun like diamonds... I began tasting—eating the crystals and licking the sap off the leaf. I went through the rows tasting different leaves. While at it, I forgot the time and the sun made its descentinto darkness. "Syamammo!" my father called out.

I leapt out of the field and stood on the boundary. "What is it, Appa? I'm here," I said.

"What are you doing, ra? Are you licking the jowar sap? Don't! It'll cut your tongue, you won't be able to eat rotte! Chilli will burn—be careful," he said.

'I know, but it is very tasty. I can't let go,' I thought.

"I'll continue a bit more. Go home while it is still light, daughter," he said. He tied the lunch vessels into a bundle, placed it on my head and gave me instructions to reach home safely. The path was filled with cowherds, and I walked with them all the way home. Mother's contract labour was over, and she came out to meet me.

She took the empty bundle off my head and asked how I fared. "Did your father scold me for sending you?" she asked.

"No mother, I told him that it was your last day at the contract. He didn't say anything."

"My daughter has my mother's qualities," she said, caressing my cheeks with both hands and then pressing her folded knuckles against her temples. Hearing the loud and ready cracking, she said happily, "My daughter always thinks about me." Weary, I fell asleep early. I don't even remember my mother waking and feeding me.

★

The cock had not yet crowed when my mother woke me up. I got up sleepily. She took me out and gave me some charcoal for my teeth. "Brush your teeth quickly and I'll braid your hair."

I wondered why—I couldn't understand anything. "Why did you wake me up now?" I grumbled.

"Don't speak loudly." Hearing my mother speak like that, I felt nervous and my sleep evaporated. As I quickly finished brushing my teeth and came into the house, I found that my father was already up. He was arranging some papers and clothes in the suitcase. I watched him, and silently went to my mother at the stove. "Have you finished, my dear?" she said, pushing the firewood into the stove. "Unbraid your plaits," she said. I questioned her with my eyes: "Why this hurry?" She pacified me with a nod. After she had tied the rotte bundle, she began combing my hair. "Such thick and long hair! How will this little girl comb it herself every day?" she muttered, and then, turning to me, she said, "Don't fight with other girls. Be friendly with everybody. Do each other's braids." I then understood that I was going to the hostel at Tandur. "I am supposed to go in two months, aren't I? Why the hurry?" I asked.

At that moment, my grandmother Sangavva woke up and spoke almost in her sleep. "The plague be on them! May they die and their waist-cord be thrown into the tree! May their eating and shitting be stopped!" she cursed. "They have been keeping an eye on us. It seems someone in the past laid a rule for our family. And we have to follow it—like a rule of god. Curse that god! Does he not have children? A lineage? What sin have we committed? They have come like Yama himself to spoil our child's life." She began weeping inconsolably. My mother leapt to Sangavva's side, held her shoulders and said to her, "This is no time to cry aloud. If you do, it will be heard and the news will find its way to the landlords. If they come to know, father and daughter will not leave the village today. Don't cry, my dearest mother-in-law. Keep your mind strong."

"Why do you cry, mother? Our god is with us and we'll go as far as we can with our strength. I'll never put my child in bondage and grief!" Appa said to Sangavva. She raised her head and looked at us. Her eyes were glowing red, and wiping them, she said, "Yes, my son. You have expressed what I feel in my belly. Such an act cannot be committed in this family. My mother, my grandmother, my great-grandmother—nobody could point a finger at them. However much the landlords insist, don't agree to this. In the end, even if they put a sword to your neck, stay true to your word. Keep the family's honour, my son."

What was all this commotion about? I didn't feel like asking them at that moment. 'I'll come to know by and by,' I thought. But my mind didn't stop wondering. I kept listening to their words. The village seemed to be thinking about me. It was clear that the matter at hand was as prickly as a thorn bush. That was why my family was so concerned. This much I understood. Then mother said, "If we sit talking about this, it will be dawn and you won't be able to leave. Go quickly!"

Appa wore his freshly washed dhoti and shirt, tied the striped towel to his head, and put the black shawl on his shoulder. He picked up the suitcase in one hand, his wire-wound staff in the other. He touched his mother Sangavva's feet. He told me to do the same. I fell at her feet too. "Go safely, my children. May your task be successful," she blessed us. My mother woke my brothers up. "Wake up, my sons. Your sister is going to the hostel. Send her off," she said and had them touch my feet. "Be careful," she said to us.

Without speech or sound, we left the village. It was not yet dawn—an hour to go. The morning star hadn't yet appeared. The Three Plough Spikes constellation was high in the sky. The moon shone bright on the path. My father walked ahead, and I followed. No, my father strode ahead and I ran to keep up with him. The path was wet and marshy. The frogs in the paddy field croaked loudly and, as we passed, they leapt back into the water with a series of plops. The snakes on the plot boundaries slithered into the fields. We had to cross the village border by dawn. We had to go beyond the Mampuru lotus lake to a bus stop a mile ahead—only then would we find a bus to Tandur. My father leapt across the field canals on the way and helped me across holding my hand, saying, "Be careful." We reached the road just as the bus came.

★

In the morning, all the girls stood in a queue with their plates in hand. My father asked them and found out that it would be some time before the warden arrived. We sat under the neem tree and ate our packed food. The warden came just as we finished. My father went to her, knelt and touched her feet with his hands and forehead. "Oh, my good fellow, why are you doing this? Tell me, what has happened?"

"Amma, you are my daughter's mother and father too. Now you alone must take care of her. We gave birth to her, but we cannot confront her fate. If you show no mercy now, my daughter's life will remain a raw wound. Everything is in your hands. We've been told that it will take two months for her name to come from the head office for admission. We don't have the freedom to wait these two months for the orders to come. We have been waiting so far, but the upper caste patel of the village have made the sinful decision that my daughter should become a jogini."

"A jogini?" the warden asked.

"A jogini is a girl from my community, the madiga community, dedicated to god."

"I know what a jogini is," interrupted the warden, but Appa continued, "The patel will take her as his woman in the name of god, with the approval of all the upper castes and the priest in the village. She will then be available to every man in the village in god's name! I brought her here without the knowledge of the elders as soon as I heard of the decision. They had heard that I was going to put this girl in the hostel for her studies. They summoned me." My father went on to narrate every detail of what had happened. "'Balappa, you son of a bitch! Sending your daughter to study, are you? Don't you know the ways of the village, you bastard? If blight descends upon the village what will we do? How dare you stop a tradition that we have upheld in this village for so long, you ignorant fool?' the landlord said. To which I replied, 'Oh

Patela, if my only daughter becomes a jogini, how can I live with myself? All the mala-madiga children in the surrounding villages are being sent to school. I have left both my sons to bondage. I would like to send at least this child to school.' The dora's eyes went red, and he said, 'Have we spoken to you gently only to hear all your lame excuses? First tell me, are you going to make this girl a jogini or not? In this village, our word is law. We speak for the good of the village. Tomorrow, we may have deaths, disease, drought or famine. To try and appease the gods after that happens would be futile. We should do our dharma—only then will god look after us. Goddess Ooradamma's festival is coming up—who will mount the stage? Who will set up the swing at the goddess Polepalli's fair? Our village's jogini, Lasmi, has become old and barren. She can no longer recite the required verses on the stage. The last time there was an epidemic of smallpox in the village, we wanted to sacrifice a buffalo, hang a strip of its flesh from her mouth and take her on the customary circuit of the village. She tried, but her legs buckled and she fainted on the boundary wall of the paddy fields. Before taking the stage at Ooradamma's festival, she was to fast from the previous day. She was supposed to climb on the pot as the oracle, and foretell the fortunes of the village. She failed. She couldn't climb Polepalli's swing either. Even younger women can't climb the swing, how could that old hag? This will not do. We have to dedicate another girl to the jogu. This should be done under the mentorship of the old jogini while she is alive, the sooner the better. We have the responsibility to ensure that an ill wind does not blow across the village. All of us have to look to this. How could you send your daughter to study without seeing to this need? If you don't do your duty and I mine, we are doomed. We have to follow what is written on our foreheads. Who are we to change our destiny? You know that the fingers of the hand are not equal, don't you, my man?"'

"This is what he said, Amma," said my father to the warden. "We have brought up these children skipping a meal every day. We are sending them to study so that they will not be bound to our slavery. How can I give my daughter away as a jogini after having watched her grow up before my own eyes? My stomach burns. I feel more dead than alive." At this, Appa choked in grief and, speechless, he began sobbing out aloud. This was the first time I had seen my father weep uncontrollably and I felt the village's lake flooding with sorrow. I held fast to my father and could not help but cry myself.

Appa wept, I wept, and the warden's eyes filled with tears. She wiped her eyes and said, "The girl is getting frightened—don't weep, Balappa. What you are trying to do is very good. Stick to your decision." My father replied, "Whatever happens to her life later, take her into the hostel now, my mother," and fell at her feet again. The warden said, "The government banned the jogini system ages ago. Don't the landlords know this? Why are they continuing with this foolish practice? All right Balappa, I'll take this girl into the hostel and send her to school. Go back and be at peace. Should the landlord tell you to bring your daughter back and offer her as a jogini, you come straight back here. We'll file a police complaint against him," advised the warden sternly.

"All right, my mother. I'll repay your favour by working for you. I'll plough your land if you need me to. As of now, I'll bring you two bundles of hay for your milch buffaloes," Appa said. She replied, "All right, bring the hay for now." My father bent double once again and touched her feet before he came out. I followed him. The warden returned to her work. Appa put his hand on my head, "This is good fortune, my child. Study well and be careful. I'll return now, and deal with the landlords." He put his shawl on his shoulder, tied his turban and strode away rapidly. I stood there and watched him go.

★

Three girls, who were clearly looking for an opportunity to speak to me, came to my side and greeted me. They became my friends. The day passed quickly in study and play, but at night I remembered my mother and brothers; Appa too. I was not used to sleeping alone.

At home, I used to snuggle against my mother's warm body. If I had to go to the bathroom, my mother would wake up and come along. When we went to bed, my grandmother Sangavva and her mother Lasumavva would regale us with stories. When we slept in the yard, we would count the stars in the sky and tell each other stories about the constellations—the Three Plough Spikes, the Golden Bed, the Hen and the Chickens, the Scorpion.

In the hostel, we told each other whatever stories we knew after dinner. I would tell the girls all the stories my mother and grandmothers told me. After that, we studied for a while, and then spread our mattresses and lay down in a row. When the watchman came and said, "Now go to bed, all of you," I would cover myself fully with my sheet, but wouldn't be able to sleep. I remembered events at home with a shudder and my stomach sank with anxiety. I wondered what had happened to my father, what the landlords had said to him, whether they had abused him or beaten him up, and how they might have made him suffer. I thought about how much my mother and Sangavva must have cried, and wept myself. I never knew exactly when I drifted into sleep as I cried. I had nightmares and would wake up suddenly, sitting bolt upright. I missed my family deeply and wanted to go back to see them.

In the morning, the mess cook asked, "What is it, my dear? Your face is swollen, your eyes are red—are you ill?" I did not reply. Not knowing what to say, I shook my head and my desire to weep increased. But I couldn't cry, because I was afraid they would say I wanted to go home and send me back. So I swallowed my tears. One day when the cook saw me all pensive like that, she inquired, "Remembering your mother and father, are you? In a few days, we'll be having a four-day holiday. Everyone will go home. Why are you so sad? You should go too." I cheered up.

On the day I had to go home, I removed my ribbons, lightly combed and plaited my hair, and tied it up in a loop. I quickly washed up, ate my breakfast and went to school with the other girls. When the evening bell rang, I put the money my brother had given me, his winnings at a game of marbles, into my skirt pocket. I put the new books that I had been given into my bag, so that I could show them to my father. I slung the bag across my shoulder and started for home.

★

It was spring and the jowar plants were pregnant with seed. Sparrows swooped, circled and dived among the plants, waiting to eat grain as they burst out of the ears. Unlike these impatient sparrows, the wise crows, as if knowing that the time was not yet ripe, flew confidently across the fields in groups.

The trial begins when the ears pop and the grain comes out. This is when a guard platform must be put up in the middle of the field. The field is just by the road, and is overrun with melon creepers. When the cowherds come, their cows will run into the field and crush the jowar plants. Passers-by will pluck the raw ears of jowar to roast as a tasty snack. So one person must remain on watch day and night in this crucial period. Now, Sangamma has a two-month job at the field. She must be there twenty-four hours a day. Someone will have to bring her meals each day from the house.

The sun was rising, and Sangamma told her son, "Balappa, arrange for poles for the platform during the day," as she picked up the broom, ready to go gather the leftover grain from the threshing grounds in different fields. "All right. We have the poles, but I need to locate sticks for the platform. I'll cut a few branches from the acacia trees lining our fields, okay?" said Balappa, shouldering his axe. He picked up his rotte bundle and set out. He hadn't yet crossed the village boundary when the landlord's bonded labourer stopped him. Balappa looked calm on the outside, but inside he was trembling as he tried to walk by. The boy, giving him due respect, said, "Uncle, the landlord is calling for you." Balappa's heart froze, because he knew immediately that he was being called because of Syamamma.

"How long can we hide a secret in a village? It will come out one day. What shall I do? What will be, will be. I sent her to the hostel fully knowing the risk, didn't I?" Balappa muttered to himself, his thoughts in a whirl. "What for, my son?" he asked. Downcast, the boy replied, "About Syamamma's going to school, what else?" As if done with his duty, the errand boy left in a hurry. Balappa was at a loss. He turned around and walked back into the village. As he crossed his neighbour and brother-in-law, Talaari Pentappa, he said, "The landlord has called me. Tell your sister and my mother," and walked towards the landlord's house.

Passers-by who already knew the bad news looked anxiously at Balappa as they crossed him. 'Only God will protect me,' thought Balappa, looking up to the sky, pressing his hands together and raising them in prayer. He appealed to the passers-by with fear in his eyes. He crossed the madiga quarter, then the mala colony, the telaga bazaar and reached the landlord's house at the centre of the village. Balappa had thought that the landlord would be alone, but he saw him from afar, sitting with the sub-inspector of police, the ex-sarpanch Chandra Reddy, the moneylender Badrappa Setu, the village revenue accountant Karnam Srirama Sharma Pantulu. The landlord's name was Anantha Reddy and he was the sarpanch of the village. The watchman stopped Balappa at the gate.

"Wait, Balappa, the elders are in a meeting," he said.

"My man, the Patel called for me. He should know that I came as soon as he called. Let him see me once, and I'll wait as long as necessary," pleaded Balappa.

"You sit down. I will tell him. They'll get angry if you interrupt them," the watchman replied.

Balappa sat at one side. In two hours, some of the people from the meeting walked away. Only the landlord Anantha Reddy and Srirama Sharma remained. They left the meeting room and came out to sit on the platform where they met the people of the village. The watchman came out and said, "Balappa, the Patel is calling for you. Come."

Balappa stood immediately, took off his turban and held it in his hand, left his slippers outside the door and walked in, saying, "Salute Patela!"

Anantha Reddy and Srirama Sharma talked among themselves, paying him no heed. Balappa folded his arms across his chest in submissive obedience and stood there, eyes cast downwards. The landlord looked him up and down and asked, "Where did you go off to, Baliga?"

"Where did I go, my lord? The jowar field is ripe for the sparrows and I was going to cut down some acacia branches for the watch platform," said Balappa.

"You are getting too clever, you rascal. This is not about today. Where have you taken your daughter?" the landlord asked, raising his voice.

Even as Balappa tried to continue, "Patela, my daughter…"

"You have answers on the ready, do you, you son of a bitch? What do you think of yourself? Do you not want to live in this village? Even though we have spoken as gently to you as to a parrot, you have sent her to study. The moment you sent your daughter to study, you disobeyed your village's order. How daring of you!" said the landlord sarcastically.

"My wife was stubborn, saying that the girls in the next village are going to school, and that her sister's children are studying too. She was the one who insisted that I send Syamamma," said Balappa, trembling.

"What lip and impudence, you scoundrel!" the landlord raged, looking around for a weapon to beat Balappa with. Finding no stick, he picked up a paperweight from his table and flung it at Balappa's face. It struck him on the forehead and blood flowed copiously. Balappa stood still. The landlord's wrath did not abate. "However much we thrash you, your kind shows neither respect nor shame," he said, and standing on the platform, kicked Balappa on the chest. Balappa fell backwards and hit the wall behind him.

Srirama Sharma, looking on, said, "Why do you beat him? It's such a nuisance! Look ahead at what needs to be done. What is the use of beating these mala and madiga, or talking to them? The government has no shame. 'Education for all' they say. If everybody is educated, who will do the work? Each person has an occupation, a skill. Our village is a self-contained republic—where the barber, the dhobi, the cobbler and the labourer … each has his own function and place. Each has to do his duty. The work of the jogini has to be done by Baliga's daughter. We have already taken this decision."

Turning to Balappa, Sharma continued, "You knew this. This obstinacy is your downfall, you wretch. What has happened to you? Didn't the poor Patel explain everything to you with the greatest patience?"

Turning to the landlord, Sharma said, "He is bleeding profusely. If he is left here for long, this place will become impure. What if he dies here? Have him sent out immediately."

The patel's labourers hurried in and picked Balappa up by his legs and shoulders, carried him out, and threw him onto the street. The news of Balappa's beating spread through the village like wildfire, and reached his wife and mother.

His mother Sangamma, hair undone, came hurrying to the spot, and seeing him, wailed, beating her chest and forehead. She clutched Balappa to her bosom and sobbed inconsolably. "You were born to me after so many penances, my son. You were never a man who harmed even an ant. How did those hands find the will to beat you? Who were the blackguards who did this? May those hands be stricken by leprosy! May robbers crush those fingers!" Muttering to herself, she cried, looking around her for something. She cradled his head on her lap, and used her sari end to press the wound on his forehead. The bleeding did not stop.

Balappa's wife, who was beside him, cried out, "What injustice is this, my lord? What sin have we committed? May we not live in this world?" She started looking around for a healing shrub. She found it behind the landlord's cowshed, brought a few stalks, and squeezed the juice on to Balappa's forehead. Even then the bleeding continued. She squeezed the stalks even more and put the crushed residue in the wound and pressed it down. Sangamma held it fast on the forehead. Balappa's wife went to the inner door of the landlord's house and began to ask his wife for some water. Even before she had completed her request, the landlady cut in, "Why have you come here, woman? If the patel sees you here, he will kill me. Go away," and banged the door shut. Balappa's wife went to the house of another landlord, Ram Reddy, who belonged to another political party, and begged at the inner door—"Amma, I'll fall at your feet, I beg you. Please give me some water. My husband's mouth and tongue are caked dry and he cannot speak. Blood is flowing like a stream. Please give me some water."

"Yes, all of you had raised Anantha Reddy on your heads, calling him Patela, Patela! All of you cast your votes for him and made him win the election. You got my husband defeated. Didn't you have any brains then? Now you come asking for water. I went to every mala and madiga house asking each one of you to cast your vote. All of you said you would. But none of you did. This is how our times have become unjust. What can we do?" said the landlady, pouring out her woes to Balappa's wife.

"Amma! Please give me some water, Amma," she reminded her.

"Water? You are asking for water? Where should I pour it? Why haven't you brought your vessel? Go! Get it now," replied the landlady.

"Amma, where can I get a vessel now? My house is far away. By the time I return with it, he'll be dead. I beg you. I am your servant. Please give me the water in some vessel," she pleaded.

"There is a toilet mug on the shelf in the cattle shed. Bring it. I'll pour water in it for you," said the lady.

Ananthamma's heart broke. She looked at the landlady's face. But she realized that it was not her moment, ran and brought the mug. The landlady poured water. As she carried the leaky mug back, all the water drained away. She flung the mug to the ground and looked around her. The doors of all the houses were shut. The reddy–komati neighbourhood was deserted. There was no chance of getting water anywhere. Just then, the mala woman Kashamma was returning from work to feed her child. She looked at Ananthamma and asked, "What happened, aunty? Why are you crying?"

"Your uncle has no water to drink: he is half-dead," replied Ananthamma.

"Ayyo! He is in such a bad condition!" Kashamma replied. Then she had a wild idea, and hesitated, looking around furtively. "We could give him some breast milk at least," she suggested. Ananthamma looked at her, speechless with gratitude. Both of them hurried to Balappa's side. Ananthamma cupped her palm and Kashamma squeezed milk from her breast to fill it up. Ananthamma carefully poured the milk into Balappa's mouth. In this way Kashamma gave seven or eight palms full of milk. They put some of the milk on the wound.

"Enough. You need to feed the baby," said Ananthamma.

"Don't worry. There will be more milk soon. But if people know I did this, my life will be hell! I'll go now," said Kashamma and hurried away into the lanes between the compound walls. Slowly, the bleeding stopped, but Balappa's eyes did not open.

★

The landlord emerged from the house after making a phone call and saw the fallen Balappa and the women surrounding him, the rusty mug on the ground.

"Where did you find the water, you bitches? Why are you gathered here as if your house has burned down?" he shouted. Turning to his labourers, he asked, "You madiga bastards, why did you let them come here?" He ranted at the women, "It is because I employ your mala and madiga men that they let you in," and then wheeled back at his workmen, "You have great love for your caste, have you? Remove these people from here immediately! Take them to the grass stacks. Leave them there and get back to work at the well," he said.

The two men took Balappa and put him near a grass stack. The women followed them and sat down. His mother called out, "Balappa! Balappa!" He stirred a little and tried to open his eyes. The women watched him, and wiped the bloodstains off his face with their sari ends. The labourers said, "God knows when the landlord will come, and when you will go home. Take this tiffin and hide it so that someone doesn't see it," and, giving them their lunch packs, left them.

★

Appa slowly opened his eyes and saw us. He saw me and tried to get up immediately. He swayed, "Amma," and fell back again. He waved me close to him. "Why did you come back, my dear? All this is for your sake!" he cried. My mother and grandmother sobbed inconsolably. I wondered why, after having beaten him so much, the landlord had had him put near the haystack. Nobody knew. Whatever the reason, my father was awake, and the bleeding had stopped. He could speak to us, and we were all a little calmer. We waited anxiously, wondering what the landlord was up to. In a while, five or six men in white khadi walked towards us, among them the police sub-inspector and the village elders. My father saw them and sank back. He then remembered what the hostel warden had assured him and took courage. The landlord too was not as angry as before. They were advancing with some papers in their hands. We saw them and stood up immediately. My father tried to stand, but fell back and lay there, as limp as the bloodstained clothes he had on him. He cried out, "Amma, Amma," and bit his teeth to try and stop the pain.

The landlord walked up and said, "Baliga, you did not listen to our words. You made me beat you unnecessarily. We all know what a good person you are. You saved my life once. Will I ever forget?" Turning to his companions, he said, "On that day in the fields, Baliga and Kurva Malliga were with me. Malliga took the cattle home to tie them up and bring me food. At that time, robbers came to steal the tuvar dal, and were filling up their sacks. When I tried to stop them, they raised their axes. At that moment, Baliga snatched an axe from one of the robbers and brandished it back at them. All of them ran away. While he turned on them, I found time to hide behind the paddy heaps. Then Baliga chased them away with his staff. He saved both my life and grain worth thousands of rupees. At that time I had called him a hero."

Turning to Appa, he said, "Now you have become too stubborn and wooden-headed, and do not listen to anyone. We are telling you this for your own good. When you live in a place, you must maintain good relations with everyone. You must listen to the village voice. You should not forget the village's command. Without thinking of all this, you put your girl in school. Even if she does study, what is going to come of it? How is she going to study alone in a different town? Times are bad now. If we settle her as a jogini in our village, she will constantly be watched over. What is there in study, Baliga? However much you study, you can't escape labour, can you? If she grows up a bit, what guarantee is there that she won't follow some man who makes a living selling tea and washing teacups? If you decide to keep your girl in school after this much has happened, it is your decision. But you'll not be permitted to stay in this village. We'll tell you what we want, you listen," said the patel.

Appa looked at the group of men, cowering like an animal in front of a pride of lions. All of the others nodded in unison, agreeing with the patel. Sangavva, standing by him, began sobbing. My mother, standing beside the grass stack, cried out, "Oh my god, my home has been destroyed!"

The elders were furious. "These women make an unnecessary racket. Kick them in the stomach. The pain will shut them up," one of them said. My mother and grandmother fell silent.

"Listen carefully. The Patel is speaking only for your good," advised Srirama Sharma, as if he were taking a class.

The patel said, "Look, we don't know what you are thinking. Until now, if we have told you to do one thing, you have done something else. If we told you something for your own good, it did not enter your thick skull. Now I'll tell you what I have decided. After this it is your choice. I asked you to make your daughter a jogini, but not for my sake. It was for the good of the village. Why is it that this fact does not enter your dull mind? I have no patience to talk to you any further! Either you make your girl a jogini, or leave the village. If you persist and stay on in the village stubbornly, you'll share Madiga Jangadu's fate. Beware!"

As soon as they heard this, my parents and my grandmother trembled. They saw before their eyes, Jangayya, a strapping young man, screaming as he was burnt to death. All the mala and madiga were grief-stricken by Jangayya's death, but no one could cry. Why? This was because the patel alleged that he practised magic, searched his hut and found turmeric, kumkum and lemons—the well-known and convenient tools of that trade. So they garlanded him with old truck tyres and set him afire in the village square. Everybody was terrified—if they cried, they too would be charged with practising magic. No one—relatives, siblings, or parents—came to his funeral. After he died, people felt that nobody should die such a death. Appa used to say so often, "Jangayya was an innocent man. Nobody could say an ill word against him. He saved money by working hard and often starving himself, and bought a bit of land. Then the patel's eye fell on that land and he killed Jangayya. Everybody knew this, but nobody spoke up." When my family was threatened with this fate, they feared the worst. My father's eyes were downcast.

"Now, without being too clever, sign these papers, and I'll write the land transfer document," said the patel.

Appa could actually write well—he was the first person who taught me how to read and write. Not only that, he was also the person who taught our community troupe a play by the dramatist Pothuluri Veerabrahmam. But he did not make any move to sign the papers. The realization that his land was being grabbed from him was such a great blow that he forgot he even knew how to write. He looked on, dazed. He had to lose either his daughter or his land. Left without an escape route, my family stood silent like puppets.

"Come on now! How long do we have to wait for you?" said the patel men. They came to my father and Sangavva, and forced both their thumbprints on the paper.

"Here—take this money for your bus fare! Leave the village immediately," said the patel, giving Appa a few green notes.

> "From now on, the red earth field will not be ours!
> The black clay field beside the canal will not be ours!
> The madiga quarter will not be ours!
> The home and yard we were born
> in will not be ours!
> The house we had built with lime and mortar will
> not be ours!
> We have become birds without a nest!
> We have become orphans with nowhere to go!"

Sangavva and my mother cried out in lament, rolling on the ground.

To no avail. We boarded the bus to town—only the clothes we wore belonged to us.

"We've suffered this fate because we decided to send you to study. We'll support you with our labour as long as our limbs are able. Don't worry, daughter. Study well and become a big officer," said my family, and this was the courage that took me through my education.

My childhood, marked by a refusal to become a jogini, and by my father losing his land, is a raw wound for my family, for my community and for me—a throbbing memory even today.

TRANSLATED BY R. SRIVATSAN

ELLAMMA IS DISTRESSED

Ellamma Daskindi

This year the grain harvest has been good. There are five bags more than in previous years. This was possible only with the blessings of Eedamma," Ellamma said as she gazed at the bags— nine rows of them—stacked so high they almost touched the rafters. Her husband, Tirupataiah, agreed. It made her happy just to look at the bags stored there in the eastern corner of the verandah. She asked him to put aside five bags of the new grain to give away as kothalu. The scent of new rice had seeped into every nook of the house. It had found its way through the gaps in the old, curved tiles of the roof and those between the hinges of the front door.

Ellamma set out to cook. She had shifted the hearth to the front yard, and placed it under the neem tree because bags of grain now blocked the passage between the front room and the kitchen. Just then, a young boy—of not more than ten years— ran up, calling out to her. He addressed her as 'Elli'. "Why sir, why are you panting? What's the hurry? Stop for a while and take it easy," Ellamma said. "No, no, I am not panting. My mother asked me to come and collect kothalu from you. Give it to me quickly, I have to go," said the boy.

Ellamma went into the house, brought out some new grain in a winnowing tray and poured it into the young master's bag.

Now he had to put five fistfuls back into the tray. She held his hand, helped him pick up a fistful, circle the tray with it five times and then drop it in. At first the boy did as he was shown, carefully and in silence. But then he stopped suddenly and pulled his hand away as if someone had slapped him. Or maybe he had just remembered a warning. "What happened, sir?" Ellamma asked, hesitating as if she made a mistake. The boy said, "My mother didn't say anything about doing this. She told me to stand at some distance from you while taking the grain."

"That's okay. You can maintain some distance. Now take this bag of grain and carry it carefully home," she said, without giving much creed to what he had said. Ellamma's youngest son was there, playing with a calf. He was fourteen and was called Malli. The young reddy boy was tempted to play with them. He stood by, watching. But he soon remembered that he had to go, picked up his bag and said "I'm going, Elli. My mother will be waiting for me." On hearing this, Malli got furious. 'What's this?' he thought, coming out of the cattle shed, 'He is younger than me and very much younger than my mother, yet this little fellow addresses my mother by her name, and that too as Elli!' He gave the boy a knock on the head, saying, "How dare you call my mother Elli? Aren't you ashamed of yourself?"

The young reddy was shocked. He couldn't understand why Malli had hit him. He ran back tearfully, nursing his head. But before he left, he warned, "I'll tell my mother that you hit me." He ran back, and arrived completely out of breath. His mother asked, "Why have you run so fast? You could have come slowly." She took the bag from his hands. He wanted to tell her that Malli had slapped him, but didn't. His mother asked whether Elli had given him the new grain from a distance or not. "I hope you took the rice without touching the old bitch," she said. She took the bag from him, placed it carefully outside the threshold and asked the son to wait outside. She then sprinkled some water on the bag of grain and also on her son. Only then did she allow him into the house. She poured the grain into a winnowing tray and asked what 'Elli' had been doing. The boy wanted to put his hand over her mouth when she said 'Elli', worried that Malli might hit her too. But then he thought to himself: 'Whatever it be, Malli is my friend in school. He sits on the front bench because he is short, but he always comes first in maths.' What's more, he used to borrow Malli's maths notebook to copy answers. If he fought with Malli now, he wouldn't get the notebook again. So he kept quiet.

"It's time for school. You'll be late if you don't leave now," his mother warned. He picked up his bag and set off. When he got there, he found Malli walking up and down as if waiting for someone. He was relieved to see Malli and ran up to him. "I've been waiting for you," Malli said. "Did you tell your mother what happened?" Malli asked anxiously. "No, I didn't tell her that you hit me," the young reddy replied as they hurried into the class, hands on each other's shoulders.

★

One by one, Ellamma had managed to get all her seven daughters married. They gave the children whatever they could afford: a goat to each of the older daughters; a cow and a calf to the younger ones. Twenty acres of land was left for the six sons. Through all this, her only desire was that her sons should not be burdened with debts and that her daughters should be happy.

She had never held back when it came to expenditure for marriages, rituals, deliveries or any other event. Beginning with the eldest daughter's children and going down to her youngest daughter's children, she had given everything she had to take care of them. She had never spared a thought for herself; nor had she kept anything she had earned for herself.

Giving birth to thirteen children, bringing them up and seeing to the cultivation of the land had eaten up all her energy, so much so that she had named her last daughter Saalamma (meaning, Enough). But then she became pregnant again. She tried all means to rid herself of the pregnancy. Someone told her eating coconut and jaggery would do the trick, so she ate a lot of that. She jumped off large stacks of grain. But however much she tried, it was of no use. That son, the one they had not wanted, is Mallanna. Ellamma and Tirupataiah affectionately call him Malli. Everyone says, "Ellamma's last son is really strong. Despite all their efforts, he survived. He's sure to live a long and healthy life." Ellamma brought up Malli as she attended to her different tasks. She used to feed him while she tended the goats; bathe him while they drank at the tank. One day Malli suddenly fell ill. He fainted. Ellamma was desperate. She picked him up, held him close and carried him into the kitchen. She sprinkled water on his face. "Go and call grandfather Ellayya," she instructed Saalamma. She herself sat by him, pleading, "Malli, Malli, my Mallanna, open your eyes, my son." With one arm, she held Malli close to her breast and with the other, she picked up some fresh turmeric shoots from the pots inside the house. Sitting before the hearth, she heated a turmeric shoot on the coals. She placed Malli on her lap and pressed the hot turmeric on his forehead. Malli jerked back to his senses and began to

wail. She rested his head on her shoulder and tried to calm
him. Then she vowed, "Eedamma, my mother, save my child
… I'll sacrifice a sheep and give a feast of thanks." Malli sat up.
Soon he was out playing—bouncing around like a ball.
Ellamma relaxed. Since then, she has never failed to give thanks
to Eedamma, every single year.

★

Even though the night had ended, dawn had not broken. It
was the morning of the day a solar eclipse was expected. It
would last for two hours. A large, auspicious, bronze plate with
a pestle placed erect in it was filled with water and placed in
the open. People were told to look at the eclipse that way—
reflected in the water. The elders said: "Whatever happens,
don't start work until it's morning gruel time." Men hesitated
to take the cattle out to graze. People stood around everywhere
in groups, chatting. Suddenly some people showed up, their
dhotis folded up to the knees, Andhra-style. They stopped
their motorbikes but did not turn off the engines, which
continued to make a 'tuck-tuck' noise. Everyone looked up.
The same question passed through all their minds: "Who
are they?" The elders knew—"Who could they be, but
Andhra guys…"

"The Andhra fellows have come! They've come to buy
our lands…"

"Look, they're wearing white clothes like teachers, maybe
they are teachers." The children gathered around them.

Meanwhile Ellamma had arrived, looking for Malli, "Hey
kids, is our Malli with you?" she asked. "Mother, let me just
finish this game of marbles first. Then I'll run and bring the

goat that was left behind at uncle's house," Malli pleaded. "That is the he-goat we set aside for god. You have to go quickly," Ellamma said. But Malli continued playing as though he had not heard his mother. Losing hope, Ellamma went to fetch the goat. It was late and the goat was hungry. It strained at the rope, ready to run on to the village road. "Cool down, stay calm and wait," she said, scratching the goat affectionately on its head and back.

Ellamma untethered the goat, picked up the end of its rope-leash and began walking back. The goat suddenly started straining at the leash. Ellamma tried her best to hold it back, but it dragged her into the group around the Andhra guys. In the mayhem that ensued, it butted one of the Andhra fellows. No one there could control the goat. They searched for Cendraiah. He was an expert at controlling cattle that were aroused or disturbed. They had to search the whole village before they found him, and brought him over to calm the goat down.

A week later, the Andhra guys returned. They rented a huge dilapidated house that belonged to the landlords and settled down there. It seemed they had come from far-off places like Guntur and Vijayawada to buy land. The money they offered was attractive, and one by one people who owned land began selling it. The reddy, the velama, even the sabbanda got in on the action. People even went to the Andhra fellows in groups, asking them to buy their lands. These transactions continued for four or five months. Soon most of the land in the village had been sold. The Andhra guys who had bought the land began cultivating it.

Madiga Ellamma held on to what little land she owned. She did not even consider selling. One day, the Andhra fellows came to meet Ellamma while she was grazing cattle in the field. They said, "Ellamma-garu, we hear you have land to sell, why don't you come to us?"

Ellamma was surprised. The reddy and velama of her village had never addressed her as Ellamma, that too with a respectful suffix. And yet these people are calling me Ellamma, she thought. A long time ago, a reddy who normally said 'Elli, Elli', had called her 'Ellamma'. Just once. That's all. It had made Ellamma so happy that nothing could diminish her joy. She thought he was going to offer her some important work. When she shared this with other mala and madiga women as they worked in the fields, they would laugh. Those memories came back to Ellamma's mind. And here were these Andhra guys calling her 'Ellamma-garu' and actually coming to her house to ask for her land. Thoughts crossed her mind: 'These people have been offering seven or eight lakh rupees per acre...'

"How many acres are you planning to sell, Madam?" one of them asked, breaking into her thoughts. She remained silent. He asked the same question again, a few minutes later. Ellamma did not respond. Assuming that she was deaf, he raised his voice and repeated the question, this time a little louder. This irritated Ellamma who had been looking north at the grazing cattle. She turned her head slowly towards him and asked: "Who told you that I would sell my land?" Then, looking him straight in the face, she asked again, "Who told you ... yes, yes ... that I'd sell the land to you?" The Andhra guy stuttered, at a loss for an answer. Without pausing, she asked again angrily: "You ran here, as if I had told you that I would sell my land. Who is the rascal who told you that I would sell the land?"

"We just asked. That is no reason for you to get so angry. It is up to you to decide whether you want to sell or not, but..." one of them began, playing for time. He continued: "Listen, Madam, in this village Erra Bitchi Reddygaru, Elamakanti Jalpapathi Raogaru, Communist Narasimha Reddy and others like them have sold us half their land. They never spoke as you are doing now. We did not expect you to react like this."

"So what am I supposed to do? If they sold off their land, they did as they wished. Don't I know your plans? If I sell my lands, my children will become wage labourers in our own fields. Is that a good thing? Tell me, what do you think? You are like Yama and his messengers, chasing after me and asking me to sell the land, sell the land... Get out of my house, get going!" Ellamma shouted. Putting an end to the matter, she walked away and moved the cattle to graze on the other side of the field.

Perhaps the cattle had also understood why these outsiders had come. They stopped chewing the cud and looked up, puzzled. Black Ox looked at the man wearing his dhoti folded up. It moved forward as if getting ready to butt him. "Stop, stop. Can't you see that I'm talking to them? There's no need to worry," Ellamma reassured it. When it heard her, it stepped back, nodding assent. This ox was like an elder son to Ellamma.

Women working in the nearby field heard the sounds and thought, 'Just think. These white-shirted folded-up-dhoti people came as a group, that too directly to the fields. Tomorrow they will be in our houses. They must have said something ... that is why Ellamma shouted like that. She never says a single word to anyone without reason, and here she is, calling them rascals. The matter must surely be serious.'

Cendramma and Suramma came up to her to find out what the matter was and to offer her support. They brought their calf along, and asked "Ellakka, do you have some betel leaves to spare?"

Seeing Cendramma and Suramma, Ellamma relaxed. "See what happened. I don't know these people. I've never even seen them. But here they are, in the fields, pressuring me to sell my lands. They give lakhs and lakhs for the land, we hear. But today they buy our lands, and tomorrow they will throw us out from our own land. They may even throw us out of this village, and snatch from us the very lives we have known. And who's to say that they'll stop at that?"

Suramma said, "Don't worry. Just tell them what you think." Ellamma relaxed a little. The Andhra fellows, who had waited all this while, understood that Ellamma had nothing more to say to them, started up their motorbikes and left. The gouda, golla, kapu and mutrasi with fields adjacent to Ellamma's had sold their land and got lakhs of rupees. But Ellamma was not going to budge.

*

Ellamma is now seventy years old. Landlords, their wives, and even their children still call her 'Elli'. She has cultivated twenty acres of land, given birth to thirteen children, raised them and settled each of them into their adult lives. Whenever a new crop is harvested, Ellamma distributes a part of the grain to the others in the village, just as the chindu give food and grain to the dakkali even before they ask for it. She gave a portion of the new rice, new green gram, and all the other crops to the mandahechu and gangireddhu people. Bangle-sellers, cloth-sellers on bicycles, those selling pots and pans, hawkers with large baskets on their heads—everyone used to wish Ellamma first, believing that she would bring them good fortune and their goods would sell better if they did so.

Whenever there is a big event at Ellamma's house—like a marriage or a birth—she makes sure that all those who work regularly with her in her fields are served toddy. She is open and affectionate in her speech. People say of her: "Ellamma's warmth is like that of the earth itself. That is why she could cultivate twenty acres of land and give birth to many children. Her house is a fertile place, bursting with children; both the house and the granary are overflowing."

Everyone in the village believes that Ellamma's hands, her feet and her words, all possess the gift of good fortune. Even people from the next village say the same thing. No upper caste woman has this gift. When a girl comes of age or gets married, her relatives call Ellamma and fill her lap with grain and fruit.

But things have changed now. Time has lost its way somewhere. Her heart is broken. She who never thought twice about taking care of thirteen children; she who had bought twenty acres of land while working as a wage labourer on reddy fields; she who never worried about what the upper castes would say when she bought the land; she who, unafraid, cultivated the land and brought up children while her husband was away working as a rickshaw-puller in Chennai; she who kept her land when everyone else was selling it off to the guys from Andhra; this same Ellamma is now tired, defeated, at the end of her tether. She had hoped that the children she had given birth to would protect the land and tend to it. But her sons and daughters are all scattered far and wide. There is no one to care for Ellamma, or of the deity of the fields and the village, Eedamma; their shrines lie untended and in disrepair. Ellamma is worried, up against a wall. She feels troubled and helpless.

TRANSLATED BY P. PAVANA

THE BOTTOM OF THE WELL

Bayi Talam

It was mid-afternoon. The wedding guests were feeling the heat. The pandal was packed and humid. Among the guests were four teachers from a nearby town. Without the fans that they were accustomed to, they felt the heat really badly. By the time the wedding was over, they were soaked in sweat.

"Why stand here sweating like this? Let's go and take a dip in the field well," one of them suggested.

"What's the point of just getting into the water? Let's buy some soap and have a proper bath," said another.

They noticed a bright-eyed young boy of about thirteen or fourteen passing by. They felt like striking up a conversation with him. One of them called him over and asked: "What's your name?"

"My name is Sangadu," the boy replied.

The teacher was surprised to hear him use a half-name, typically assigned to lower-caste people by their employers. He wanted to discuss it, but changed his mind; the occasion was not appropriate for such conversation.

He turned to the boy and asked, "Is it ok if I call you Chinnoda? Would that hurt you? Would you mind if I did so?"

The boy's eyes lit up. The teacher could tell that he preferred the new name. "Chinnoda, can you buy us a piece of soap?" he asked, handing over some small change.

'What an honour it is to run errands for educated town people,' Sangayya thought to himself. He sped off to the nearby shop as if he was in a race and brought back a cake of soap in no time.

"Oh … we wanted something larger. This won't be enough for the four of us. Could you go back and buy us a bigger piece, or maybe two of this size?" one of them asked.

"This was the only piece in the shop and the shopkeeper gave it to me."

Since there was nothing else they could do, the teachers decided they would wash their bodies with water, and use the soap only on their oily faces.

"Which well should we go to?" they wondered.

"Devakanyala Bayi," Sangayya replied.

"Where is that?"

"It lies to the east of the village. Come, I'll take you there." He led the group of teachers to the well. Several boys were swimming there. One after another, they climbed the iron frame of the pulley and dived in. It was obvious that some kind of competition was on. The teachers walked up, their eyes riveted on the boys.

Sangayya pulled the marbles out of the pocket of his loose cotton shorts, and put them into his shirt pocket. He then hung the shirt on a nearby tangedu bush, pulled up his shorts and tucked them into his waist-string. Then he too climbed up the pulley frame, stretched his arms out straight and dived into the well. The teachers were struck by the way this young boy swam—as naturally as fish, they thought to themselves. The other children raced each other, swimming in circles. Some of them played the 'catch me' game, others, a 'cock and hen' game that these teachers had never seen before. Two boys faced one another. One of them said, "Cock or hen, choose." When the other had indicated his choice, he pressed the tip of his middle finger into his thumb and struck the water as one would a marble. Sometimes it would make a 'koko' sound, like the cock, and sometimes a hen's 'kaak' sound. If the sound was 'koko,' whoever had chosen 'cock' would catch the first boy by his head and dunk him in the water. If the sound was 'kaak,' the boy who chose 'hen' would get to do the dunking. The boys swam with abandon. It looked as though there was no limit to their enjoyment. Every once in a while they would return to the sides of the well to take a breathing break, but would soon return to their games.

There must have been about fifteen or twenty boys in the well that day. Only the older and more experienced boys played 'fetch the mud from the bottom of the well'. Of the three such boys, our Sangayya was one. These boys would dive to the absolute bottom of the well, pick up a fistful of sand or pebbles and rise to the surface. Sangayya, who had been playing with all the boys until that point, looked around, as if searching for someone else. Just then Sammayya floated past, right in front of his eyes.

"There you are! I've been looking out for you. Shall we play 'bubbles'?"

Sammayya nodded in agreement.

They shouted out to the other boys, "Can you guess which one of us is going to come up first?"

This game was a favourite with everyone. The smaller children moved out quickly, leaving only the two bigger boys in the water and stood by watching, their faces lit in admiration: these boys were, after all, their leaders. They were keen to know who would win the game today and whose head would be pushed down into the water for having lost the game. Pentayya, who was waiting by the edge with his fingers in his mouth, ready to blow the whistle and start the game, asked "All ready?"

To the watching teachers, Sangayya and Sammayya seemed professional swimmers, like great sharks in the sea. They were certainly as skilled as the experienced coaches in city swimming pools. As soon as Pentayya whistled, the two boys who were facing each other dived down to the bottom of the well and sent up a bubble each. The bubbles expanded as they rose to the surface and burst with a big 'tup'. Each boy had to come up alongside his own bubble. The one who emerged first —and before his bubble burst on the surface—would be the winner. Today, Sammayya won. The boys broke out into a cheer. A second later, Sangayya surfaced. "Yesterday Sangayya was the winner and today it is the other way round," someone observed. They shouted for the winner to grab Sangayya by his head and dunk him into the water. Bubble game over.

"Children, don't go away. But do not jump into the water either. Allow the waves to settle. I am going to give you some 'milky bubbles' today!" shouted Bijjaram Cendranna, who was slightly older than these boys and who had arrived smoking a bidi. They stayed on to watch the show. Cendranna placed the lit end of the bidi in his mouth letting the other end jut out into the water. He dived down to the bottom of the well on one side and surfaced on the other side blowing out the smoke from his bidi all the while. The bubbles emerged in a half-moon, bursting one after another ... tup, tup, tup ... and releasing the white smoke. "Ho, ho, ho! Look at the milky bubbles!" The children clapped and shrieked with pleasure.

Watching the children, the teachers from the town forgot all about their bath. What accomplished swimmers these children are, they thought. Sangayya was just about to climb up the pulley frame to dive into the water again, but hearing the teachers call out, he stopped and walked towards them.

"Who taught you to swim?" one of the teachers asked.

"I taught myself," replied Sangayya.

"But someone must have taught you the first time…"

"My grandfather used to float palm trunks in the water for us. I used to tie them to my waist and practice every day. After a while, I was able to let go of the logs and began swimming with my friends."

"Do you boys swim every day?"

"Yes, about seven or eight of us get together and take our cattle out to graze. By midday, the cattle have usually had their fill, and having drunk water from the ponds, they lie down in groups under the trees to rest. That's when we begin our games in the well."

The teachers felt a bit foolish for asking them about swimming lessons. It seemed a bit like asking the fish how they learnt to swim.

"Unlike town kids, these kids don't have swimming pools or coaches to train them or even Dunlop tubes to serve as floaters," commented one teacher.

He turned to Sangayya, "Will you teach us to swim?"

"Uh … come, we'll teach you," replied Sangayya and ran towards where Lame Mogulappa, the watchman at the paddy field, was sitting. He pulled off the turban cloth from Mogulappa's head and tied that to the teacher's waist. He and another boy holding the two ends of the cloth stood on two sides of the well and one of them said to the teacher: "Now jump into the water. Don't be afraid. Just paddle. Push the water with your hands towards the underside of your belly. Try not to swallow it."

The teacher listened to the boy like an obedient student and jumped into the well. The swimming experts continued to give more instructions, but the teacher couldn't hear them. He began sinking… He bobbed up and down in the water and was swallowing it. Having noticed that the situation was going out of control, the two boys dragged the teacher towards the steps of the well so that he could sit and catch his breath. Sangayya came up to him and said: "It's always like this the first time. If you practice every day, you get better gradually."

Realizing that it was quite a while since they had come to the well, one of the teachers said, "Let's go. If we don't get the direct bus to Hyderabad, we'll have to change two buses and also walk nearly three kilometers. We should hurry. Besides, we haven't eaten yet."

The four walked down the steps of the well. The one on the step closest to the water held the soap and the others waited their turn to wash their feet and their faces. On his way up, the first one bumped into the soap-holder accidentally. He steadied himself, but the soap slipped from his hand and fell into the water.

"Ayyo, the only piece of soap we had is also gone," cried that teacher, looking at all the others who were now worrying about having to go back to town with greasy faces.

Sangayya, who had already dried himself with his shoulder towel and was putting on his clothes, heard the commotion and asked, "What happened?"

"The soap fell into the water."

"Where?"

"Here. It fell from this step, on this side."

"When did it happen?"

"A minute ago, maybe."

"Oh, in that case, it would not have reached the bottom yet."

"How do you know?" asked the teachers.

"We play that game 'bringing the mud from the bottom of the well' every day…"

Sangayya stopped buttoning his shirt, pulled it off over his head, jumped into the water and raced down along the path of the soap, which had almost reached the bottom of the well. The teachers kept looking anxiously at their watches and at the water. Three minutes, thirty-four seconds. Sangayya surfaced with the soap in his hand, and gave it to the teachers who just stared at him in wonder. Having been in the water for over five minutes the soap had worn thin. The teachers waited no further. They washed their faces with soap and their feet with just water.

After they were done, one of them commented: "How clever these children are!"

"It's a smartness that grows out of their rich experience," said another.

"True," the third agreed.

"If such talent and worldly knowledge were to be supplemented with education, how much better it would be…"

"Why is it that town children, despite being educated, lack this kind of creativity and practical knowledge?" wondered one of them.

"Not all village children possess these skills; not all of them are creative, helpful and so on. This boy who bought us the soap … he didn't know us at all and yet how helpful he has been. Isn't that out of respect for us and our education?"

"I think the environment into which one is born, and the kind of life one leads, determines one's creativity and talents. The boys who tried teaching us to swim, the one who retrieved the soap from the well, are all cowherds. They don't even own the cattle they are looking after. My guess is that they work for someone else who owns the cattle for a small wage."

"It is true that not all village children are this spunky."

"You surely don't think the land-owning people's children, and those from the upper castes, look after cattle to earn daily wages. I did not see any of them at the well..."

"I think these children are certainly dalit children ... maybe they belong to the mala and madiga castes," said one of the teachers.

They decided to ask Sanga—no, we must say the full name —Sangayya or Sammayya.

Those two were trying to coax the buffaloes lying in a pool of slush to come out by prodding them with sticks. The teachers walked towards them and asked, "Which caste do you belong to?"

"We are madiga," said Sangayya. "Baindla," Sammayya elaborated.

The teacher who had guessed the caste of these children gave his friends a knowing look—as if to say, "See, I was right."

TRANSLATED BY DUGGIRALA VASANTA

A BEAUTEOUS LIGHT

Deepasundari

At the crack of dawn, Ellamma was out taking her herd to graze. She had named each buffalo, cow and calf in the herd. Calling out to each by its name, she gathered them together and set out with them on their daily round. Every day, the herd would drink its fill of water from the Mahesha tank before it moved into the surrounding pastures. Ellamma did not need to shepherd the flock at all. She never even had to shout 'hey' or 'ho'. As soon as they were out of the shed, the cattle would walk swiftly towards the tank. The fast-paced buffaloes and cows were followed by their bouncy calves, all eager for a morning mouthful of water.

The sun pushed its way into the eastern sky. Taking ritual dips in the clear water, an ashram inmate prayed to the crimson head emerging from the womb of the sky. He was alone at the Mahesha tank—it seemed as though he had strayed from his ashram crowd. His name was Somasekhara Sharma. Exactly at that time, the herd of animals pushed its way into the tank. Ellamma stopped on the bank. Hearing them, the praying brahman boy turned around. He looked anxiously at the animals. Afraid that the beasts were heading towards him, he screamed and moved away from the edge of the tank right into the water. His feet slipped and he fell. Beating at the water, he cried out desperately: "Oh mother, oh father, I am going to die."

The herd continued to drink, oblivious of the commotion. But Ellamma picked up those barely audible cries for help. She looked to see who it was ... nothing except a little movement in the water, and bubbles rising to the surface. At first she thought it might have been caused by the herd. 'But I did hear a human voice...' She scanned the water more carefully. She caught sight of something white moving in the water, some distance from the herd. Then the screaming brahman boy surfaced, only to sink again. As he was going down, his arm came up, as if gesturing for help. By then, it was clear to Ellamma that someone was drowning in the tank. She yelled, "Ayyo, someone has fallen into the tank!"

Quickly she tucked up her long skirt and half-sari into her waist-string, tied her hair up into a knot and prepared to jump in. Somewhere at the back of her mind, she heard her mother's voice cautioning: 'Stop, my darling daughter, Ellamma.' She paused for a moment and thought, 'If I jump in, surely my hair will get wet and mother will be annoyed. Father doesn't like me doing such things either. I'll catch a cold. They would assume that I simply made up this story to swim in the tank. I need to make sure that my hair remains dry. But what about this person? He will die if I don't come to his rescue. What is the way of pulling him out without getting my hair wet?' Then a thought flashed through her mind.

Looking around, she called out, "Dopati!" Lazily grazing in the soft sunlight after having drunk its fill, Dopati sensed the alarm in Ellamma's cry. It stopped grazing and cantered up to her, swishing its tail, pricking up its ears and nodding its head, as if to say—'I am ready'. Her clothes and hair in place, Ellamma jumped on to Dopati's back, legs astride. As if on cue, Dopati moved into the water. The brahman boy looked as if he had swallowed a lot of water. His voice was weak. He was desperately waving his arms. Dopati swam swiftly towards him. Ellamma shouted out: "Grab the tail, hold on to it..." Desperate to hold anything that he could, he managed to catch Dopati's tail, but couldn't keep his grip. Ellamma, astride Dopati, stretched out her leg, but he wasn't able to grasp it. She could see he was slipping away. His arms refused to move. He looked ready to pass out.

Then, Ellamma tried to pull out Somasekhara Sharma herself. It was not easy. She tried to catch him by his hair, but there was only a tuft on his head. The flow of water made it difficult to get hold of the tuft so she grabbed his sacred thread. But that got tangled in her fingers and broke. Even his waistcloth had worked loose. She decided it was time to take a drastic step. With one hand she caught his tuft and with the other, held onto Dopati's horn. She signaled to Dopati to swim back to the edge of the tank. While Dopati swam, Ellamma, still astride on its back, dragged the boy through the water. Since he had swallowed a lot of water, he had grown heavy. But Dopati bore the weight and Ellamma managed to bring the boy to the edge and drop him there.

Still sitting on Dopati's back, she rode forward, crying out for her father. Everyone working in the nearby fields heard the cry, sensed that there was something wrong, and lifted their heads to look. Ellamma, half-sari around her waist and hair tied up, was still on Dopati's back. Fearing some danger, they shouted, "What happened, Ellamma?" She could only say, "Come ... come soon." Several men and women working in the red gram and rice fields gathered around immediately. Her clothes were dripping wet. Women pulled her down from Dopati and hugged her. They patted her face, head, hands and legs dry with the edge of their saris.

Ellamma pointed to the boy she had dragged out of the water. They were shocked at what they saw. A light-skinned boy lay spread on the black soil. His loincloth had been washed away and had reached the other bank. He lay there, absolutely naked and still. The men went closer to check whose child it could be. They turned his face towards them and peered at him. They wiped the dirt off his face. "It's a boy from the ashram," they said in astonishment. They wrapped him with one of their turbans, moved him from the edge of the water and laid him on the ground. The boy's stomach had swollen like a balloon. The men turned him on his stomach and pressed down on the small of his back. They did this till he had brought out all the water that he had swallowed. Others tried to figure out which family he belonged to. "He is the son of that big-bellied man in the agraharam. He is called Sharma or Varma," someone said. Others said, "Whoever it is, let us carry on." The women wiped his hands, feet, hair and head dry with the ends of their saris and rubbed his hands and feet to warm them.

A raw motku leaf was rolled into a cigar and was filled with vaama husk. It was lit with fire made from jekumuki stones. One of the men pulled the smoke into his mouth and blew it out into the boy's ears. His mouth and nose were also similarly filled with smoke.

Meanwhile, finding it difficult to stand there wet and dripping, Ellamma had returned home with her herd. Worried, her mother Manikyamma came up to her. When Ellamma told her what had happened, she stared at her, terrified and her eyes filled with tears. Hugging Ellamma, she began to weep. "What if something had happened to you in that tank? What would we have done? It is our luck that our daughter is back safe.

What if suddenly…" Ellamma's father, Adivaiah, who had been listening intently to her story till then, scolded his wife, "Keep quiet! You are scaring the child with your wailing. Move over." He circled a salt-filled hand around the daughter's head to drive away the spirits who might have been getting too fond of her, and threw it into the wood stove. "Well done, daughter. Don't pay any heed to your mother's words. She is just an idiot." He turned to Manikyamma and proudly declared, "My daughter saved that boy's life."

To Ellamma he said, "Go and change into fresh, dry clothes." He put on his chappals, wound his shoulder towel into a turban around his head, and picking up a big lathi, walked straight to the Mahesha tank. The brahman boy was sitting up. Trying to recall everything that had happened, he described how he had begun drowning and how terrified he had been. His voice was low, so the words were difficult to pick up.

As soon as he arrived, Adivaiah asked, "How is the boy? Is he alright now? Has anyone sent word to his people? Do they know he is here?" Someone said, "We've not seen any of his people. So we couldn't tell them." Adivaiah responded, "So what? It is our responsibility to convey what happened." Matangi Rajayya said, "If even one of them had been around, we wouldn't have to go to their place. I hope we can spot at least one person."

Cendraiah joined in: "Why would they come this way? They do not need to set up the plough or water the fields. They must be relaxing on chairs in their front yards, playing with their sacred threads, taking care not to disturb the food in their bellies. There's no way they will be found here. Someone will have to go and tell them."

Adivaiah intervened: "The boy must be hungry and thirsty. Whatever he had eaten would have come out when he was turned on his stomach. He will need food."

He turned to the boy and asked, "My child, do you want to eat something? It may take a while for your people to pick you up."

"How can the boy answer such a question?" Poshamma commented. "Look, Sangamma is making leaf-cups for goat's milk. He can have some of that. But first he should be given some honey."

"Babaiah, why don't you go and get the bottle of honey hanging from our rafters? The children will not be able to reach the bottle." Even before Adivaiah finished his sentence, Babaiah was on his way. Within no time, he returned with the bottle.

Adivaiah peered in the direction of the agraharam to check if anyone was coming their way. They caught sight of two people in the distance, and a buzz arose from the crowd, "They can give the news to the agraharam." "They have turbans on their heads, lungis folded up to the knees and blankets slung over their shoulders." "They are carrying something on their heads and are holding something long in their hands."

But Adivaiah countered them, "They can't possibly be from the agraharam. They are our people. You can tell from their swift, long strides—as if someone were chasing them. A brahman stride is never so fast. They don't need to walk quickly to the field, or match the canter of the calves. They always chase others, no one ever chases them. Our metari, Matangi Muthyalanna, seems to be walking in front. Yes, now that they are here, I remember. Last night, a buffalo died in the karnam patel's house. All the madiga metari went there to move the dead buffalo. They must have gone in the early hours and returned only now. They seem to have bathed and changed into fresh clothes after cleaning their knives in the stream."

Adivaiah relaxed after he recognized Muthyalanna, "He has come at the right time. This boy seems really frightened. We can depend on him to soothe the child with his mantra-tantra. We can relax now."

Muthyalanna saw the commotion and called out to his sister-in-law, Poshamma, from a distance, "Why is everyone gathered here, leaving the work in the fields undone? Did something unfortunate happen?" She replied, "It looks like you already know everything. This boy from the agraharam was drowning in the tank and is frightened. Come and take a look at him." Muthyalanna walked towards Adivaiah. "Brother, so you are here too? I couldn't recognize you in that blanket."

The crowd parted to make way for him. He sat down to examine the boy. First, he placed his hand on the boy's head and pulled up the eyelids to check for redness. Extending a shoulder for the boy to lean on, he laid him out on the ground. Gently rubbing the boy's lower side of his abdomen with his palm, he pulled the flesh up towards his bellybutton. The boy let out a low scream. Soothing him with an encouraging, "Bear the pain just this once," Muthyalanna poked his three fingers into his belly button. The boy screamed again. But Muthyalanna continued to hold his fingers firm. Next he turned the boy over onto his stomach to examine his back. He felt the neck, shoulders, ribs, thighs, knees, calves, feet and toes with his hands and said, "He is fine. It is good you people made him throw up the water he had swallowed and purged the body of damp. But the boy is still in shock." He recited a mantra and slapped the boy on his back. He then walked up to the nearby water-pump, saying, "Get me a cup of honey to feed the boy while I wash my hands and feet. I came here straight after cutting up the dead buffalo. My hands and clothes are still splattered with its blood." He rubbed hard to clean the dry blood off his nails. Then he heard someone saying, "This boy refuses to swallow honey. However much we try, he keeps his mouth shut tight, his eyes too..." Muthyalanna responded, "This foolish boy will collapse if he doesn't eat. Force his mouth open and pour some honey in. But be careful. If he gags in the process, his life will be in danger." To this, a voice said, "What is it we can do to force the honey down his throat? He is as soft as a dung-worm."

Muthyalanna pleaded with Poshamma to give him some honey. Dipping his index finger in the leaf cup, he chided: "You fool, open your mouth." The frightened boy did as he was ordered. "Put your tongue out," he added in the same stern tone. As the boy put his tongue out, Muthyalanna touched it with his honey-dipped index finger and instructed him to swallow. The boy obeyed. After four or five sips of honey, the boy felt better and licked his lips with his tongue. "Lie down now." Muthyalanna threw the leaf cup aside and instructed the people around, "After a while, give him fresh goat's milk. He'll recover. Then take him to the agraharam and leave him there."

Poshamma gently reminded him, "We will do that. Why don't you wash off the dried buffalo blood from your hands?" Muthyalanna, walking towards the water-pump, said defensively, "I had to rush to make this boy swallow the honey with the bloodied hands. I was worried he would fall into a faint. Now, I'll clean myself thoroughly and also wash my clothes."

Soon the boy was strong enough to sit up. He drank the goat's milk. His face came alive. He stood up and began to move around. The madiga sent him off on a bullock cart along with a burly young man. He stopped the cart at a distance from the agraharam and asked Somasekhara Sharma to alight. "We've reached your house. You can go now." Sharma stumbled trying to alight from the cart. The residents of the agraharam heard the cart and saw a weakened Sharma staggering out. Some of them came forward to help him but stopped in their tracks when they spotted Madiga Bhumaiah. Bhumaiah lifted Sharma up and sat him down on a rock below. He had expected Sharma's parents to rush up to the cart, but there was no trace of them. He wondered whether they knew what had happened. Instead of rushing off to tell Sharma's parents themselves, the residents of that quarter who had gathered around the cart asked Bhumaiah to call out for them himself, as if it were his mistake not having called them earlier. Bhumaiah called out loudly, "Amma … Aiyah." "Louder," they said. He called out louder. Then they turned abusive: "You dumb, untouchable fellow, don't you have a voice? Call out loud." He obeyed. But they scolded him again, "They are not your mother or father. Call them 'devuda, swamy'." Bhumaiah cursed them under his breath. "These idiots don't know what they are saying. They tell me to call out and then scold me when I do so. What do I do now?"

Meanwhile, an old man in a dhoti and no shirt came running out. His beard and sacred thread were of the same colour. "You untouchable, why did you shout? Tell us what you have to say, quickly." But, after noticing the whole neighbourhood gathered around the cart, his mouth went dry. He stared at Bhumaiah stupidly and shouted, "You fool, just tell me what happened."

Bhumaiah began, "This young brahman boy..." Narasimha Sharma interrupted him impatiently, "Which young brahman, tell me quickly." Bhumaiah rapidly reeled out the facts. "Your young brahman boy fell into the tank. Our Ellamma rescued him." Then he turned the cart to return to his wada. The shocked Sharma went quiet for a moment. Hearing the sounds of bells from Bhumaiah's cart, he yelled, "You! You untouchable, why can't you tell me clearly? How did my Somasekhara Sharma fall into the tank? Where is he now?" Bhumaiah pointed, saying, "There he is, sitting on the rock," and drove off in his cart. Narasimha Sharma ran towards his son and was about to fold the exhausted boy in his arms when Subramanya Sharma stopped him. Meanwhile, Rukminamma, the boy's mother had also arrived. With tears in her eyes, she stood beside her husband. He turned to her and wailed, "Look at the condition of our boy." Anguished, she replied, "This is written in our fate... Can we hold the boy, can we touch him now?" The others warned: "No, not yet. You can touch him only after he has been purified through the shuddhi karma. Now let us do our work." Both the parents stepped aside, but their gaze stayed unwavering on their son. The boy had become even more distressed. Fear engulfed him now. The elders of the agraharam brought fire, water and a pujari in special clothes for the process. The pujari stood at a distance and told the boy to shut his eyes. He chanted mantras as he poured water on the boy's head and tonsured him. He stripped off the boy's loincloth and threw it into the fire. Then the boy was made to walk around the fire. The boy's stomach had started rumbling. The honey and goat milk had all been digested during the time-consuming shuddhi karma. He felt dizzy. Finally, the process came to an end, with Sharma's tongue being touched by a gold wire heated in the holy fire. He closed his eyes as the wire was taken out of the fire, but the moment it touched his tongue, he let out a scream. With this, the first phase of shuddhi came to a close. It was decided that Sharma's family would be isolated from the community for a week. It was an established practice to keep such families in a separate room in the agraharam if such pollution had taken place. When the exhausted Sharma collapsed on the bed in the designated shuddhi-house, he was given a tumbler of curd. With that, he fell into a deep sleep.

★

It was mid-afternoon. On the threshing floor freshly harvested, pearl-white jowar seeds were being winnowed. But the process was held up because the breeze was moody and dropped often. Cendranna, the eldest son of the family, head covered in a kerchief, his winnowing pan filled with jowar, stood waiting for a strong gust. His mother, head wrapped with the end of her sari, was sweeping the chaff off the mound of jowar with a pulivayili broom. The breeze remained halting, with long gaps in between. Manikyamma thought to herself, 'If the wind were steady, we'd have been done with this job by evening.' Tired of waiting, Cendranna put down his winnow, picked up an empty basket and used it to fan the chaff off the pile of jowar. Meanwhile, Manikyamma's ears picked up the sounds of a distant song. It came in gusts, along with the wind. Her daughter-in-law asked, "Who is that, Atta?" Manikyamma replied, "Who could it be but Kasamma, the middle daughter-in-law of Bairedla Bhimmanna. She sings such amusing songs. Anyway, the wind is back, give us the winnows." Everyone went back to work. As the wind gained strength, the song grew clearer. The afternoon progressed and the shadows grew longer. It was as if the song was being sung right next to their field.

Manikyamma said, "If you had joined in with the refrain, she would have continued singing. Why don't you at least sing now?" Yerra Sammakka, who stood next in the line, said, "Since it's getting dark, let us not start with a lengthy song. Let's sing a short funny one." Manikyamma thought: 'Everyone is tired after the day-long work. If we sing, we'll all feel more energetic and the work will be done sooner.' So she said, "Come, my daughter-in-law, sing along with me."

Early in the morning, the madiga woman
                              goes to the village lake
to collect firewood and dry leaves.
Early in the morning, the brahman comes to bathe;
asks her to scrub his back.
'I am scared of your pot belly.'
'Let me cover it with a cloth.'
'There's a dead bull in the kapu house,
why don't you bring it for us?'
'A young and innocent brahman I am,
how would I bring you the dead bull?'
'Go and get us its liver and its heart.'
'A young and innocent brahman I am,
how can I bring you the dead bull?'
'I'll give you sharp knives, young man,
small as well as large, young man.
Cut them out and bring them here—
small liver for my small aunt; big liver for my big aunt;

and with the small intestines, let us cook a sweet curry!'
'A young and innocent brahman I am,
how can I cut up a dead bull?'
'Oh you, lentil-eating, milk-drinking brahman,
how do you like the taste of this curry?'
'Great! Let me have some more, some more.'

It was dark by the time the jowar had all been winnowed. The grain was filled into sacks and the ends stitched up. What remained was poured into the baskets. The leftover grain on the threshing floor was carefully swept up by mother and daughter. The sacks were loaded onto carts. Everyone—men and women alike—worked together to get the harvest done. They had spent the entire day in the field. The jowar crop had been very good. It was celebrated with mutton and toddy. In the evening, the cartload of jowar was taken home. Adivaiah's eldest son walked ahead of the cart, holding onto the yoke. The younger son drove the cart. The women followed, carrying the baskets and all the different measures.

Adivaiah's family was known as peddintollu—the big madiga household. If you asked around, you would be directed to the house of the peddamadigollu. When the sabbanda caste people came to their house to invite them for something, they would place the vermillion mark not only to the couple, but also the leather-curing urn. Waiting for a daughter, the couple gave birth to seven sons. Finally, when they got a daughter they named her Ellamma. Ella means always, and they hoped she would always be with them. Since she was the last child and was named after the deity, the brothers and their wives also brought her up with affection and care. The sons and daughters lived in the madiga wada whereas Manikyamma and Adivaiah set up their household along with the daughter near the field-well.

★

The sun had gone down. The animals that had been grazing on the green grass and eating the jowar hay drank their fill of water from the pool. Then they sauntered into their shed and stood beside their respective posts. Adivaiah fastened them to their posts and chopped the jowar grass into fine pieces to feed them. The buffalo was given a large amount, since it was going to be milked. First, he washed its udder clean with plenty of water. Then its calf was left to suckle. After nuzzling at the teats for a while, it suddenly butted at the udder. The mother stopped grazing, turned to the calf and tried to calm it down, as if to say, 'What is it, Idimbi, my child? Are you angry with me?' The calf continued to nuzzle, unmindful of the mother. The udder grew full and firm. Idimbi began suckling. After a little while, Adivaiah gently pulled it aside and fed it some tender grass. After Idimbi began nibbling the grass, Manikyamma started milking the buffalo.

It grew completely dark. Ellamma lit an oil lamp in their hut. Her body was itching all over from the dust of the jowar chaff. She lit a fire to heat water in a large vessel. Soon the water was hot. She poured it into another vessel and carried it to the bathroom built of closely woven vayili branches. It was a moonless night. Nothing could be seen except the stars in the sky. Inside the bathroom, it was pitch dark. Ellamma remembered that the castor oil seed that she had ground for the lamps was over. It had been a busy day in the field, and she had forgotten to replenish the stock. With the light from a bundle of gongura sticks, she ground the seeds on the stone. Wrapping the powder in a piece of cloth, she lit it with the gongura lamp. Quickly she made six more castor oil lamps with cloth. She put one in the cowshed and another on the stone next to the water container in the bathroom. Then she felt that one lamp-stick was insufficient and lit the remaining three and put them up on the projecting bricks in the bathroom.

The lamps threw a circle of light in the bathroom. Ellamma sat in the centre of it and poured the hot water over her head. Then she mixed raw soap-nuts with black clay and rubbed it into her hair. Manikyamma, who had come in to help her with the bath, rubbed a mixture of jowar powder and dry turmeric all over her body. Her daughter's back felt smooth as a petal. She drank in the sight of her child, standing there, luminous, in the golden hue of the castor oil lamps. She was overwhelmed. It was as if the Goddess Ellamma herself had entered their home. Like her, this Ellamma too glowed with beauty from a thousand angles.

★

In the light of the morning sun, the white rice-flour patterns—muggu—in front of the hut sparkled like silver. Manikyamma, who was still drawing it in the eastern corner, suddenly remembered that she had left the milk on the stove to boil. She put the muggu container aside and rushed to the stove. The milk had boiled over and had put out the fire. The hut was filled with the smell of charred milk. Trying to light the fire again, she forgot about the muggu and got absorbed in the cooking. Except for the place in front of the kitchen, the entire yard was filled with outlines for the pattern. 'Let Ellamma finish the pattern when she wakes up,' thought Manikyamma. The earth that had been wetted for the muggu had begun to dry, but neither of the parents felt like rousing Ellamma.

Finally, Manikyamma said to her husband: "We need a muggu at least in the eastern corner. Once the mud dries, the powder won't sit well; it will blow away. Why don't you wake Ellamma up?"

"Why do you want me to wake her up just for this silly muggu? No one is going to punish you if a little part of the muggu in the front yard is missing," Adivaiah responded. Ellamma woke up to the noise of the exchange and jumped out of her bed, saying, "Father, what is this talk about punishment?" She ran out and quickly completed the muggu in the front yard.

★

The agraharam reverberated with the news of Sharma's rescue. "Madiga Elli pulled Somasekhara Sharma out of the tank; she dragged him out when he was drowning; she touched him, no, she dragged him by his hair; that Madiga Elli touched our boy…"

Within a few hours, the news spread through the whole village. The agraharam, and the ashram school were both enveloped in the flames of a crisis. There were discussions, debates and analyses. More information was sought about what happened at the water tank. It was learnt that the metari, Matangi Muthyalanna, had given Sharma honey without washing off the blood of the dead bull from his hands. Everyone thought that the agraharam had fallen on really bad times.

A massive debate ensued about the ways of cleansing a brahman who had been touched by an untouchable—and that too, a woman. Search was initiated for the appropriate rituals and the propitiate moment for the conduct of the rituals. The shastris, pundits and acharyas were all on a mission to find ways to cleanse Sharma. No one spent much time thinking about how and why it had happened, they were concerned only about what should be done next.

★

Grazing over for the day, the herd came to the Mahesha tank for its daily fill of water. Having drunk, they climbed out onto the bank, sought out shadowy places to rest and settled down, chewing the cud and ruminating on the day's find. The calves sprinted around their mothers, swirling and swishing tails, foolish smiles on their faces. There were colourful cows and shiny buffaloes; there were black cows and white cows. Daamaramogga was a white cow with a black circle around her neck. From a distance, the black mark looked like a snake.

Dopati, the buffalo, had slid into the tank and was swimming around. She looked like a queen bathing in her private lake. Between strokes, she gazed at the sun setting in the west and the moon rising in the east. Branches of the trees around the tank peeped into the water. Country sparrows, woodpeckers and pigeons had all come out to watch Dopati, the swimmer. 'Why is she so headstrong? She doesn't like either the green grass here or the yellow dry grass, but goes to the jungle to eat the choicest tender grass. She scares away both the cows and bulls. Even tigers hesitate to attack the herd in which Dopati is present. She is so independent. She can easily climb big hills and mountains too. Her eyes sparkle with a strange light.' Dopati finished her leisurely swim and climbed onto the bank. She gave her body, her tail and her ears a fierce shake. Drops of water from her tail and ears splashed onto the bird nests. She found her way to the black rock that looked like a sleeping bull, near which Somasekhara Sharma was seated. She stood there in the afternoon sun drying out her body. Soon the other cows and buffaloes—Idimbi, Malle Sendu, Daamaramogga, Rangasaani, Sita and Surpanakha—joined her and took up positions near her.

Somasekhara Sharma was seated on the rock, his feet dangling in the water. There were fish of all colours in the water. He watched them swim by in shoals. They played amongst themselves and even touched his feet once in a while. A small fish nibbled at his left foot. He quickly drew it up, but soon put it back in the water. It turned into a game between him and the fish and he began to laugh joyfully when he managed to evade it. Suddenly, all the fish vanished. Where had they gone?

He looked around and found that they now surrounded a young woman who stood in the middle of the tank. She was playing hide and seek with the fish. The tank would be quite deep at that point. But this woman moved around with ease, playing and singing in five-meter deep water. Then she stepped out of water, moved up the bank and parked herself beside the mogali bush with her feet in water. Why did she sit there? She seemed to be looking for something; first she gazed at the sky, and then into the water. A parrot flew down, perched on her shoulder and gazed at the sky. Many other birds also seemed eager to watch the sky. Even the small snake in the mogali bush crawled out to gaze at the water and the sky. The herd of cows and buffaloes also joined them.

Sharma wondered what they so eagerly waited for, and began to imitate them. The moment everyone was waiting for finally arrived. The circular, crimson sun was blazing in the west. Exactly on the opposite side, the tender-light moon rose in the east, poised in the middle of Dopati's horns. It was as if the sun and moon were having a conversation, standing opposite each other in the sky, wondering which game they should play. Everyone—woman, parrots, pigeons, snake and the herd—watched the drama in the sky. Then they all turned their gaze down to the water. The water lay absolutely still. It looked as though the sun and the moon had entered the water and were standing side by side. Even the fish were still. The distance between the sun and the moon in the sky just disappeared when they were in the water. And look, there was Ellamma, sitting right between the sun and the moon. When the water moved, the sun and the moon moved too, playing hide and seek, or maybe kabaddi. The birds, cows, buffaloes, snake and woman had gathered there to marvel at the spectacle. Sharma felt overwhelmed by the moment. After nine minutes, the sun went down and dusk set in. The darkness increased gradually. The moon glowed brighter. It appeared majestic—like a woman who had just won a game of kabaddi.

She was talking to the moon and laughing. Dazzled by the mirthful woman, Sharma wondered: 'Who is she? I've seen her somewhere. The memory of her is strong, very strong … I know her, I'm sure I've seen her somewhere. But why does she not look at me, even once?'

He called out to her, "Oey, oey!" She did not bother to turn around. He thought, 'Maybe she cannot hear my call.' But he could not stop staring at her. After a while, she stopped her conversation with the moon and walked towards the herd. As if they had been waiting for her arrival, they gathered around her. She chatted with them, touching the bells around their necks. She discussed the spectacle of the sun and moon and giggled. But she was still searching for someone. Sharma wondered who she was looking for—the whole herd was gathered around her. Then he saw Dopati slowly walking up. Moving gracefully, eyes sparkling, she stopped right next to the girl. What would happen next? Ellamma leaped onto her back and sat astride it.

She walked some distance forward, then, turning in her tracks, came back and paused beside Sharma. Still seated on Dopati, Ellamma extended her hand to him. Without a thought he placed his hand in hers. She gestured to the space behind her on Dopati's back, inviting him to mount. But, while Dopati climbed up the steep bank, Sharma slipped off her back. He screamed in fright, "I am dead!" But Dopati continued to move forward.

★

Sharma woke from deep slumber and sat up. 'Could it have been a dream? If so, what a dream it was!' He wanted to live forever in the world of that dream. He remained seated with his eyes shut tight. 'Was it only a dream? I wish it were true. Didn't she drag me out when I was drowning? Yes, she did. She also visited me in my dreams, and even in the dream, she was walking in the water.' He shut his eyes again and willed the vision to return. The memory was sweet. It made him feel warm and peaceful. The weariness that had enveloped his body and his heart disappeared. He wished he could remain in the dream, seated on Dopati along with the girl. The dream was over, but wherever he turned, he imagined her presence. Slowly he forced his eyes open and glanced around. The room was old, dilapidated, dusty and full of cobwebs. Did they banish me here? He closed his eyes in fear and tried to slip back into the dream-world. But she remained in his vision, whatever he did. 'What beauty! What compassion! What a smile! Luminous in the light of the full moon! With the speed of lightning, she came to my rescue when I was drowning in the tank. In my dream too, she was luminous like lightning when she extended her hand to pull me onto the buffalo, moving along with the birds, the animals, the sun and the moon. She is Nature's own beauty. Only the very fortunate may see or talk to her. When she saved me she returned me to a new life. If so, doesn't my life belong to her now? She is my life. She is also my dream. Yes. She is my life and my dream.' Saying all this quietly to himself, Sharma rose from his bed. Without quite realizing what he was doing, he slipped out of the room, stepped out of the shuddhi nilayam, descended the steps of the agraharam temple and set out towards the madiga wada. The agraharam residents assumed that he was going for his morning ablutions. Workers on the road between the agraharam and the madiga wada noticed, but chose to ignore him. They wondered where this weak pujari child was going, but did not utter a word. He crossed each wada and finally arrived at the madiga wada. As soon as he reached there, he settled under the neem tree in front of the elder's house and sat there, leaning his back against the leather-curing urn. He gazed at the tree and the house, but soon his gaze spread in all directions, as if looking for someone.

People who spotted him from a distance wondered about his sudden appearance in the wada. But they whispered among themselves and did not approach him directly. The boy continued to look out. Soon he was identified—"This is the boy who fell into the tank. He would have died had it not been for our Ellamma." The children of the wada gathered around him to stare. It was beyond anybody's guess why he had landed up here. Matangi Muthyalaiah, just emerging from his house, holding a glass, inquired, "What are you all doing here?"

They replied, "There is a brahman boy sitting here."

"Are you crazy? Why would a brahman boy sit here?"

"Why don't you come here and check?"

Muthyalu found Sharma seated there, leaning against the curing urn.

He recognized the boy immediately. The boy still looked quite weak. "How are you feeling now?" he inquired. "Did you have something to eat?"

Sharma didn't reply. He was engrossed in looking for something.

Meanwhile, the agraharam discovered that Sharma had vanished from the shuddhi nilayam. His parents searched for him everywhere in and around the agraharam. Soon the news of his arrival in the madiga wada reached them. They sent servant-messengers immediately to fetch him back. The messengers reached the madiga wada in no time. They stood at a respectable distance from Sharma with folded arms and addressed him in a subdued tone: "Sir, your father wants you to return. Please come with us now. We'll go."

There was no response from Sharma. He showed no sign of having heard what had been said to him. They repeated their plea a little louder this time, "Sir, let us go. Your father will be angry with us if we don't take you back." This time, Sharma shook his head and said firmly: "I'm not coming."

The servant-messengers were shocked. One of them dashed to the agraharam to convey the message.

"Just drag that fool of a boy back here," they were ordered by the elders of the agraharam. Four more servants from the agraharam now arrived at the madiga wada. They informed the madiga elders: "We will lift him and carry him away." The latter calmed them down, saying, "There is no need to do any such thing. He will agree to return and you can all walk back." A large crowd of adults and children had gathered around Sharma by now.

Work in the madiga wada had come to a standstill. Ploughs remained unharnessed. Those on their way to the fields and pastures halted, along with their animals. Women, drawing muggu in their front yards, fetching water from the tank, or caring for their children, continued with their tasks, but kept an eye on the affair around the neem tree. Annoyed with the crowd obstructing his view, Sharma asked them to move aside. Not satisfied with that, he climbed onto the platform and resumed the search with his eyes.

Unmindful of his antics, the servant-messengers stepped closer and repeated their request: "Sir, your father wants us to return you to the agraharam. Even if you resist, we were ordered to carry you back. Will you come with us voluntarily or should we resort to force?"

Oblivious to their pleas, Sharma remained engrossed in his search. He behaved like a crazed person. The servant-messengers readied themselves to physically carry him. They put their lathis down by the side of the urn, tightened the kerchiefs on their heads and folded up their lungis. One of them tried to hold Sharma up by his arms, as one would pick up a baby, but the other servant-messenger gave him another idea: "There's a better way of picking up a person. You should put your arms around his waist and sling him over your shoulder." The first one bundled Sharma onto his shoulder and began to march towards the agraharam. Undeterred, Sharma persisted in looking out from the servant's shoulder. Suddenly, he let out a scream and the servant stopped in his tracks. "Stop and put me down!" His voice was ecstatic. The servant's grip loosened and Sharma slipped down. His face and eyes glowed with the joy of discovering something after a long search. He moved to his left.

Startled by this sudden turn, everyone waited expectantly. A group of young girls had gathered at a short distance from the curing urn. Ellamma stood with them watching the commotion. Sharma walked towards the group. Initially the girls wondered who he was staring at. When it became clear that his gaze was focused on Ellamma, they made way and gathered behind her in a group.

His hand outstretched and his index finger pointing at Ellamma, Sharma continued to march towards them with purposeful strides, with servant-messengers, children, madiga, mala, washermen, barbers and the rest trailing him. Ellamma folded herself into the circle of friends. Two of them put their arms on her shoulders, as if to support her. Sharma came to a halt in front of her and stared. The crowd too stared in shocked silence. The chatter subsided. There was silence all around. The messengers began to sweat. A flock of pigeons came to rest on the neem tree, flapping their wings. The tension of the moment broken by this sound, the messengers said, "Come, Sir, your father will be upset with us." Ellamma turned in her tracks and darted into her house. Her friends followed her. Sharma now seemed to have reached a decision, and one could see enormous joy on his face. He shouted, "I will marry you."

The messengers were shaking with fear. They begged him to accompany them. The madiga had fallen silent. After Ellamma left, Sharma followed the servant-messengers quietly, as if he had fulfilled a huge and responsible mission. The servants didn't need to plead with him or pick him up forcibly. He walked behind them with a new energy. But even before he reached the agraharam, a diktat had been passed against his entry. Sharma heard it, but was not perturbed. He stood there, confident that they would change their stance. But he did not receive any invitation. Noon, evening ... still no sign of reconciliation. One messenger had already left, pleading that he was hungry and needed to grab a bite. The other one stayed behind.

Tired and achy, Sharma dropped down on a stone behind Kummari Sooramma's house. Passers-by pitied his fate and hoped that he would receive a call from the agraharam. Sharma crossed over to the kapu house in the neighbourhood and asked for some drinking water. But they pleaded with him with folded hands, "Please do not ask us for water." The scene was repeated in every wada—the potters, the weavers, all pleaded with Sharma not to put them in trouble by asking for water. After a fruitless journey through every wada of the village for water, he finally arrived at the madiga wada.

By this time, the news of Sharma's declaration of love for Ellamma not only reached the wada and agraharam, but also the bungalows of the reddy, the komati-bazaar and all the kapu households. The village boiled with anger. But no one could figure out whom to argue with, let alone quarrel with. Everyone was in the habit of approaching Narasimha Sharma to get an auspicious date for an event, but now, when his son declares love for a madiga girl, what is one to do? Pondering over this, the reddy elder Ramireddy, the komati elder Krishna Gupta and the kapu elder Parandhamaiah proceeded to deliberate with the karnam patel, Varaharao. Each of them occupied their designated place on the mattresses in his front room. The karnam's face looked weighed down.

Silence reigned while each thought hard how to begin. Krishna Gupta broke in impatiently, "Our young Sharma might have gone behind that girl … but shouldn't the madiga have the sense to discourage him? Also, now if the boy goes there with this kind of proposal, what will become of the twice-born dharma? The madiga have already become quite arrogant. With this, they will think no end of themselves." Ramireddy joined in: "But we still have them in our control, don't we? Each one of them should be tied to a tree and flogged." Parandhamaiah also could not stop himself: "Their arrogance knows no limits now. They should be hacked to pieces."

The karnam, Varaharao, spoke last. "One can go on giving such speeches. But what we need right now is a plan of action. Everybody is clearly pained, but this is not the time to vent our anger. Maybe we should seek the opinion of the other elders too." They trooped out to the community hall in the agraharam. The elders of the agraharam had already gathered there to discuss the issue. The kapu, komati and reddy elders joined them. Varaharao gave a discourse on the philosophy and current political economy of caste hierarchy, lest the others stray from the issue: "Narasimha Sharma is in distress. We should extend our support for him to gain the mental strength to withstand the tragedy that has befallen him. Let me explain a few things. Ages ago, we became kapu as a result of the labour of our great-grandfathers. Now we have all moved higher in the varna hierarchy and become kshatriya. We have a strong hold on education and wealth. We have managed to keep mala and madiga out of state power with our raw strength and our hold on other resources. We should protect our interests at any cost. The only difficulty is that we cannot do agricultural work. It is they who have to till the land. We have managed to keep their wages low and have managed to exercise control by banishing them to the outskirts of the village. If we kill them, who will do the agricultural work? The land will remain fallow. To keep our village flush with food and resources, we have to try and keep the madiga and mala where they are now. They know how to till the land, to tend the animals, to prepare animal feed and raise different crops. We can't do the work of fertilizing the crops; it is they who should do it. They don't know how brilliant they are at their work. We should make them work and not let them run away."

Vishnu Shastri of the agraharam picked up the cue and elaborated. "Yes, times have changed. What you say is true. If we want our religion, the temple and our lives to carry on in the current course, we cannot do without agricultural wealth. For this, the wada is essential. If we hurt and destroy them, we would be destroying our own agriculture and wealth. The right course of action is to make sure they know their place, to keep them outside the village as untouchables and make them do all the work of animal husbandry and agriculture. We also need them to take care of our health needs. We should make sure that they do not get any new ideas and that they stay as they are now."

Varaharao concluded the discussion: "If we want everything to go on smoothly, we cannot just kill them. We should keep them in awe of us and far from the village. But we lose nothing if we get rid of the polluted person from our midst. There shouldn't be any hesitation in doing so. However, it is unwise to obstruct the functioning of the existing system for his sake. It is our duty to uphold the law of caste."

★

Sharma no longer looked out for anything. He remained there, seated on the platform, calm and collected. He was obviously hungry, but no one broached the subject of eating. Although the wada people were aware of his presence they did not make any attempt to speak to him. After a while, he went to Poshamma's house and requested water. Poshamma glanced at Muthyalaiah, Adivaiah, Narsaiah and Sangaiah—the group of madiga elders seated under the neem tree. "Why do you hesitate to give him water? Go ahead and give him some," they urged. She ran into the house and brought a tumbler of buttermilk for Sharma. He drank it and went back to the platform. After a long time, he slipped to the ground and lay there, fast asleep.

By this time, all the madiga had learnt that Sharma had been banished by the agraharam and that after this banishment the entire village refused to serve him drinking water. The agraharam was boiling and the village was in fear. Each wada feared that they would be banished from the village. But the madiga wada harboured no fear of banishment as they had always lived in banishment. As a matter of fact, they took care of all who sought shelter after such banishments. The mala and madiga elders decided that it was time to confer with the community on this issue and gathered under the neem tree.

"This is a battle with the village as a whole. The mala and madiga alone are not enough to wage this battle. Let us call the dakkali, chindu, maasti, baindla and byagari elders too. We'll send word that they should return from wherever they have gone to participate in the discussion at the madiga wada near the Naagulu pond by the evening," declared Muthyalaiah. Poshaiah readily agreed: "Yes, if Dakkali Balaiah, Chindu Narsamma and Byagari Anthaiah are around, our burden will be halved. Especially if Dakkali Balaiah is there, we can stop worrying. He speaks with such conviction that the dora and the agrahara brahman pee in their pants when they hear him, the bastards."

Muthyalu responded cautiously, "Let's focus on what to do now. We can watch who wets their pants later. All the madiga elders should come to the meeting. Even those who are bonded to the kapu should come. Lasumamma, who articulates everything so clearly and precisely, should be invited. Please gather here after the lamps are lit in the evening."

People who had gone out of the village for work quickly finished it and returned. By dusk all had gathered around the rachchabanda, the village square. Babaiah tried to clean the street-lamp darkened by soot and ash. Muthyalu told him to hurry up: "Everyone is here and we should start the meeting now."

Muthyalaiah opened with the following comments. "You all know what we have gathered here to discuss. We have a crisis on our hands, caused by this young brahman boy. He was rescued from drowning by our Ellamma and then came to the madiga wada seeking to marry her. This is why the agraharam is angry with us now. They have the support of the reddy, komati and kapu communities. Their council has taken the decision to banish the boy. Not only that, they want to teach the madiga a lesson. In a while from now, they will send out the messenger with a dappu. We'll be asked to respond. I urge you all to think about how we should act now."

Chindu Narsaiah responded, "Elder brother, can I say something? I'm much younger than you, but please hear me out." Adivaiah urged him to continue: "We are here to talk and to listen to each other. Out with it." Narsaiah continued, "We should not have let the boy come into the wada; we should not have let him sit here till the messengers arrived. We should have tied him up and dumped him back in the agraharam."

Someone intervened, "Didn't we send him off? We didn't tie him up, but our boys took him back to the agraharam, didn't they?"

Sangaiah began to speak. "What can we do if someone lands up here by a quirk of fate? Have we ever said no to anyone who has come seeking our help, whoever it be? We are the jaati who hid Ellamma in the curing urn. Didn't we stop the kamma when they were chasing Kurma Mallanna? Does a tree throw away a person who has taken shelter in its shade after a long walk in the blazing sun? Did we invite that Sharma? He landed up here. We didn't even greet him."

Manemma intervened. "What you have all said is fine. But this boy doesn't just sit here. He wants to marry our Ellamma. That is why the village is in turmoil. What kind of elders are you? Why can't you discuss the issue at hand? Are you going to get them married? Or are you going to get rid of the boy?" Others nodded in agreement.

Cendraiah responded impatiently, "Of course we know what we have to discuss. Is it so easy? Do you think discussing issues is as easy as fetching water from the lake? Go … go … fetch water."

Dakkali Balaiah said, "Whether it is easy or difficult, what she said is correct. That is what we should be discussing."

Cendraiah responded quickly, "We can discuss it as much as we want. But the point is, can we speak to them? They won't even let us sit in front of them. We have to convey our point through the mediators. The mediators don't understand what we try to say. They even get angry when we talk. You are the only one who can win them over in a discussion."

Balaiah, tapping the ash off from his bidi with his index finger, looked at everybody in an amused way, "What is there to say now? When did you ever listen to me that I should talk now?"

Byagari Anthaiah responded, "Balaiah, why do you say that? Did we ever refute what you said? It's true, we don't always comprehend what you say. Even when you speak like that, your words infuse us with courage. But we tend to be practical and think that your ideas are not workable, though we have never said you are wrong. If we live today with some strength and courage it is because of you dakkali people. We all know that. This year, as soon as the harvest comes home, we'll have a performance of the dakkali Jambavapuranam right in the middle of the village. That should silence the bastards."

Jogu Lasumavva intervened, "How is it that we remember the Jambavapuranam and Chindellammakatha only when the madiga and mala are in danger? These performances should be held every year without fail."

In a deep voice Balaiah began: "We are not blaming you. But as our Jambava Grandfather said, it is only when you prosper that all of us who are dependent on you'll also prosper. As long as you live as slaves to the brahman and the castes below them, you cannot prosper. We have always told you this.

You are the matanga kings. You don't need to be slaves to anyone else. Have you ever given consideration to our argument that you are kings? You don't know who you are. We know it. Why do you think we declare this each time from the platform in the village? Because your ways of dealing with birth, death, gods, traditions and animals are entirely different from those of the brahman. We acquaint you with your greatness, but you choose to follow the brahman despite their ill-treatment of you. This way, neither will you prosper nor will you let us live. Not only your jaati, but our jaati will get weakened. It is time you became conscious of all this. You don't need them. They need you. You should understand that."

The elders all listened thoughtfully. A silence reigned, like thick darkness.

Then Byagari Anthaiah spoke. "Though the village enslaves you, you seek our well-being. That provides us with the determination to live. The village cannot claim our lives forever. In future, we are going to have our say. No one can stop that. But tell me something. I believe some of our women saw the brahman pick up the coin thrown by the dakkali man. This year, having seen this rare event, they became the lucky ones. I wonder when I'll be able to see that spectacle... But isn't it strange that we don't know about your arrival in the village whereas that brahman who communicates through the madiga gets to know and manages to pick up the coin? Next time you arrive, you have to inform us beforehand so that we can watch this spectacle too!"[2]

---

2. This is a practice in some Telangana villages. The dakkali elders would throw some coins onto the side of the path and the local brahman would wait to pick them up. This was usually done out of sight of the other castes; madiga who perchance caught sight of the spectacle—demonstrating the superiority of the dakkali in relation to the brahman—were considered fortunate.

Dakkali Balaiah responded, "Don't worry; you can see it this year. Why do you speak about the past? Let us discuss what to do next."

Bagaiah stopped him, "Balaiah, you have always said that there is a difference between them and us. Now it is due to this difference that we landed up with this problem. Please explain to us what these differences are so that we understand them."

Balaiah replied, "Good that at least now you want to understand all this. Let me explain." Everyone's attention was on Balaiah. "If you discuss workmanship, they discuss eating; if you worry about how to live, they talk about the next birth or heaven after death; when you mention the plough, they speak of the rishis' kamandalam; if you talk about the earth, he talks about the sky; you enjoy chicken but he longs for asafoetida; you value the buffalo but he worships the cow. Why? You raise the calf into a bullock, break it in, and domesticate it for agricultural work. When it has done the work, you take care of it as though it were a younger brother: feed it the choicest grass, carefully mixed drink, a bottle of arrack sometimes, and jowar cooked soft. They keep chanting 'cow' because they extract from it butter, ghee and milk. You raise bullocks because you do agricultural work and turn the land into a productive asset. But there is no natural connection between the world in which they live and the tilling of the land. That is why they never mention the bullocks or chant the name of the buffalo. While you keep saying 'Bullocks, agriculture and work,' they keep chanting 'The goddess cow, milk, yoghurt and food.' You have Ellamma, Poshamma and Mysamma but they cling to Vishnu and Parashuramulu. They know these differences and understand the implications. You should also deliberate in the light of these differences," Balaiah said in a deep tone.

Muthyalaiah sensed something moving on his right and turned to see what it was. Others too turned their heads. Somasekhara Sharma had risen from the platform and was approaching them. He halted near the gathering and folded his hands.

"Young man," Muthyalaiah said, "The things you did have resulted in major crises for the madiga keri. Do you understand what you are doing? You are throwing us into flames. You should remain in the ashram. If you behave like this, you'll land us in deep trouble. Whatever it is, you should return to the agraharam. They'll perform shuddhi and accept you into the community after a while. And that would be a great relief for us."

In a flash, Sharma lay prostrate on the ground in front of them. He wept and pleaded, "I beg you, please do not ask me to return. Please get Ellamma married to me. Or else, you can kill me or I will commit suicide."

Poshamma scolded him. "You seem to have gone mad. Why would we kill you? If we get Ellamma married to you, we will be killed—do you know that? Do you think if you declare your wish to marry her, it will be done, just like that? Shouldn't she be willing to marry you? What if she says she does not want to?"

Sharma tried to gather strength to respond to her. Despite his best effort, no words came out. He fell unconscious. Soon this news also spread to the agraharam and the village. Adivaiah sat there, stupefied by what was happening. His head was buzzing with a hundred thoughts. 'My daughter is being pulled away into an unknown place by someone—into a bottomless pit, a dark cave… How can this brahman boy insist on marrying her? Is this some kind of a mirage? Is he a good man

or a madman? Is my daughter going to walk a thorny path?'
Tears welled up in his eyes. Ellamma had never seen her father
crying. Noticing this, Muthyalaiah consoled him, "Adivi!
Please do not get anxious over this. Ellamma is not merely your
daughter, she is a daughter to all of us too. Let us wait and see
what happens. What's new in all this, anyway? Whenever
something happens in the village or the agraharam, we surely
get affected. This time its effect is even more direct. Didn't
Dakkali Balaiah explain things to us just now? We'll be very
careful. Don't weep. And please do not get worked up. Think
about what we should be doing now."

Though Muthyalaiah's words were intended for Adivaiah,
others also listened to them keenly. By then people of the
madiga wada were joined by those of the mala wada. The
gathering resembled thickly strewn grain on the threshing
floor. Ellamma was part of the group. She stood next to her
mother, who was weeping uncontrollably. Manikyamma's three
daughters-in-law tried to calm her, along with the other
women, but she was inconsolable. Beating her palms against
her head and her chest, she wept aloud. In the middle of it all,
Sharma lay in a heap, unconscious. Ellamma's five brothers
contained their anger and tears with difficulty. Ellamma was
devastated by her parents' grief. It was because of her that the
boy was lying there; because of her that the entire madiga and
mala keri was gathered around him. What was going to happen
now? Seeing them in that state, she felt all her strength draining
from her; it was as if her body was being dismembered. She
stood transfixed.

Muthyalu took charge. "We'll hand over the boy to his
people now. This time none of the young boys should
accompany him. Narsaiah, Cendraiah, Sooraiah and I, the

elders of the mala and madiga, will go. The young people should stay behind."

A bullock cart was quickly yoked and the elders were on their way, along with the boy. The bullocks started out from the wada, their bells tinkling. The cart entered the village and went past the centre. The tinkle of the bells could be heard all through the village. In the agraharam it was heard as though it was a message from the madiga wada. People suspected that something was about to happen. The bullocks were going at such a speed that the unconscious boy was tossed around in the cart. Fearing that the boy may die, Sanganna slowed down the cart.

The sound of the bells brought all the Sharmas and Shastris out of their respective homes. Adjusting their sacred threads and upper cloths on their shoulders, they hurried out. The madiga saw them gathering from afar. Muthyalu said to Sanganna, "Let's just go straight there and hand the boy over quickly." Sanganna turned the cart towards the gathering. The bullocks slowed down and the sound of the bells softened.

Before the cart could reach the brahman gathering, a reddy, komati and kamma mob appeared suddenly from another direction and blocked the path. The men shouted, "Orey, stop. Can't you see that we are waving for you to stop? How can you just rush inside like this? Have you plugged your ears with something, bastards?"

Sangaiah continued to inch the cart forward. He had not heard what they were saying above the sound of the cart. The bullocks continued to move at their own pace. The bells on their necks beat an eerie rhythm. Unable to keep standing in the path of the moving cart, the crowd gave way. The madiga elders alighted. They were about to lift the unconscious Sharma down from the cart when they heard Vishnu Sharma's shout.

Everyone fell silent.

"It is not necessary to take him out of the cart. Reddy, Gupta and Rao tried to stop you to tell you that. But you didn't heed them. You will have to make reparation for this offence. Now you take him back the way you brought him here. This is our collective decision. There is no need to say anything more on this subject."

Reddy added more harshly, "Now that you have heard what they said, you may go. The brahman spoke to you directly, which is more than you deserve. If you delay one more moment, you'll see broken heads and bloodshed."

Dismayed by this turn of events, the madiga elders fell silent.

Gupta said, "What are you gaping at? Didn't you understand what was said?"

Unable to comprehend what was taking place, Muthyalu asked, "What can we do with this boy? Why are you asking us to take him?"

Varahararao replied, "He is one of you now. He does not belong to the agraharam any longer. It is up to you whether you want to raise him or kill him. Now, without further delay, turn your cart around and go back to where you belong." Recovering from the initial shock, the madiga elders looked at each other. Everyone now knew what would happen if they stayed any longer. As soon as Cendraiah and Muthyalu said in unison, "Shall we return now?" Sangaiah turned the cart around. Muthyalu saw the boy's father Narasimha Sharma in the crowd, trying to catch a glimpse of his son. Then he turned deliberately away and stood with his back to the cart. Muthyalaiah and Sangaiah thought to themselves, 'These people do not care even for their own. How will they think of people like us? Let us not stay here a moment longer.' As soon as they crossed the agraharam, they sped the cart towards the wada. The whole wada was out in groups, waiting for the cart to return. "Let us first sprinkle some water on his face. After that we can decide what to do." They sprinkled some water on Sharma's face and when he revived, he was given a glass of buttermilk, and made to sit under the neem tree.

People who had gathered there began wondering, "What kind of human beings are they? How can they discard their own child? Just because he took water from our houses, they threw him out. Now that he has been abandoned, what do we do with him?"

Leaning against the leafless tamarind tree, Lasumamma mumbled, "What choice do we have? Let him stay here. If he is given something to eat and learns to work, he'll survive among us." Pushpamma, who had come to visit her mother, prodded her. "Lasumavva, why don't you say it aloud?"

The elders and their deputies all waited keenly to hear what she had to say. "Why do you all get so worked up about the boy? For the past two days, no one has paid any attention to their work. Everyone is anxious, struggling like birds in the catcher's trap. You have done everything that you could. But his caste elders refused to accept him. What would happen to the boy if we also refused to accept him? What kind of human beings are they? Of course, there is nothing new in all this. Their acceptance is always conditional. Earlier too people who have been thrown out by them have lived here, eating what we gave them. This is nothing new for us. The dog which cares for its puppies is better than these people. Sharma may not have been born here, but he is a child. He'll grow up here, along with our children. As for his marriage, if Ellamma is also willing, we can get them married. If not, he'll marry another girl. Let us not worry that a brahman cannot be married off like a madiga. One of us will adopt him on that occasion. Let him stay with us. He'll learn to handle the bullocks and practise agriculture. And if he can't learn those skills, he'll become a beggar and go away."

Silence reigned.

No one had been at peace till now. But Lasumavva's words calmed them down. They felt as though after a long walk in the sun, they had reached the shade of a tree. The men, women, children and old people gathered there felt they had finally got something to hold onto. Women dried their eyes. Everyone—mala and madiga—relaxed in the scented breeze of the newly blossoming neem tree.

Lasumavva urged them to move on, "What do you say, Dakkali Balaiah, Chindu Anthaiah? Why are you quiet? What else can we do now, my sons?"

The dakkali and chindu elders said, "This seems sensible." The rest agreed immediately. Lasumavva urged the crowd, "One of you, please feed this child. As for the others, the bullocks are waiting for you. Our work has been stalled. The calves are starving. Now just grab something to eat and take them out to graze."

TRANSLATED BY A. SUNEETHA

GOGU SHYAMALA'S WORLD

Aapu
a water plant dried and used for thatch

Agraharam
the brahman section of the village

Avva
generally grandmother; in some Telangana districts (such as Nizamabad) also mother

Bantu
a servant; sometimes can be prefixed to a person's name, as in 'Bantu' Pentappa in "But Why Shouldn't the Baindla Woman Ask for her Land?"

Begari
a mala caste who work in graveyards and cremation grounds.

Betel leaf processing
on a fresh washed betel leaf, soft edible lime, which is generally sold in balls (sunnam kayalu), is applied and a little kasu is added. Kasu makes the mouth red. The leaf is then folded and chewed. Those who can afford it also add betel nut, cardamom, clove and coconut flakes to make it more sumptuous. When women meet during breaks from work , they chew them together after meals.

Bhoodan movement

it was started by gandhian Vinoba (Vinayak Narahari) Bhave (1895–1982). Inspired by a tour of Telangana districts in 1951, Bhave invoked the gandhian notion of trusteeship and asked landowners to feel compassion for the plight of the landless and donate one-sixth of their land. Unlike serious land reform, this scheme had the government's support and yet was a failure, with invariably barren and disputed land being transferred to the landless.

Brahman

priests, landowners; today bureaucrats and professionals

Chedugudu or kabaddi

a popular sport that has now gone international, chedugudu involves two teams of seven members, each occupying two equal halves of a rectangular field. A 'raider' from each team makes a foray into the opponent's side, holds her breath while keeping up a chant of 'kabaddi, kabaddi', and aims to 'touch' or 'tag' as many of the opponents as possible and reach back the field's midpoint. Each tag counts for a point. If the 'raider' is overpowered by the opponents, she is considered 'out' and the opponent scores. Being a contact sport that underscores the importance of touching and physically wrestling with other persons, the game has implications for castes that considered themselves 'pure' and resent the touch of others.

Chindu Bhagotam

the Chindu Bhagotam is a dramatic performance of a series of stories by the chindu, a sub-caste of the madiga. The chindu are primarily a performing community, a specific culture with closed family groupings that practice the Bhagotam. This performance has one story for each caste—starting with the Ellamma and Jambavapuranam for the madiga, they perform

Mala Chennaiah for the mala, then tales pertaining to the golla, the Pandava myth for the mudiraju, the Beerappa myth, etc. These are performed in different cheri and wada according to caste. These origin stories are owned by specific communities as markers of their identities.

Curing urn, landa
a large clay urn that is dug into the ground. It is filled with water to which lime, tangedu bark, etc. are added, and the animal skin soaked for curing and processing. The leather is used to make dappu, footwear, bokkenna, water containers, straps, whips and a variety of other things.

Dappu
a leather drum made and played by the madiga. The skills of madiga drummers and their powerful drums are legendary. The dappu is also played for ceremonial occasions and festivities (jatras, marriages, deaths) and during village theatrical and dance performances. Today dappu are a presence at all political meetings. Traditionally the dappu was used for village announcements (dandora) and was an instrument of communication from the rulers (kings/landlords/modern governments) to the ruled. However, with the rise of the Dandora movement (Madiga Reservation Porata Samiti, MRPS) in Andhra Pradesh in the mid-1990s, it has been transformed into a symbol of assertion and of solidarity among the various madiga castes. The message now is in the opposite direction—from them to upper castes and ruling groups.

Devuda, swamy
ways of addressing a priest; sometimes just an exclamation indicating Lord/God

Dora
the most powerful landlord in the village, the power centre. The dorasani is his wife. In contemporary times the dora

may also be the sarpanch, the contractor, or the MLA (the intermediary between the government and the people) while his sons are engineers, doctors and lawyers. The dora, the karnam and the priest comprise upper caste power in the village.

Erpula, Jogini, Matangi, Yesa, Baindla

traditionally the erpula (soothsayer) was a woman from the baindla caste. The baindla are the priests of the untouchable castes, usually very few in number—maybe one family in a village. Among the upper castes, the erpula woman is seen as a kind of prostitute, but among the subaltern castes she is seen as a priestess—a contradiction. In rural temples and in the temples of goddesses (Mahankalamma in Secunderabad, for example) the erpula woman is an oracle and a highly respected figure. In the temples of male gods, and in pilgrimage centres —Tirupati, Yadagirigutta, etc—there is no ritual function for the erpula woman. She is only "god's wife". Technically speaking, matangi is the generic name for a madiga woman. A jogini is a woman who is dedicated to temple service from the madiga caste. Jannah, erpula and yesa are regional variations of the term jogini and refer to a lower caste woman who is declared as the (sexual) property of the whole village. Jogini are usually from the baindla caste. All matangi are not jogini—some are forced to become jogini in the particular situation of non-availability of erpula from the baindla caste. Over time, this process of leaving women to the temple (like goats, sheep, etc.) has become a culturally accepted practice not only for the madiga, but also the BCs ('Backward Classes') or sabbanda castes. In such cases, especially when the 'donation' is made to pilgrimage centres devoted to male gods, the jogini, in the absence of any specific ritual function, respectability, and economic sustenance, may become a prostitute.

Gilli-danda

a game that requires two sticks and an open ground. The gilli is the shorter stick tapered at both ends, and the danda is the longer stick with which the gilli, placed in a spindle-shaped hole in the ground, is hit. When the gilli is caught in mid-flight, the striker is considered 'out'. The game can be played with two players or more, and the rules are flexible.

Jaati

while the use of the term 'caste' may suggest an unshakeable, sanskritic hierarchy; jaati refers to many communities that may be fuzzy and not always easily identifiable in the caste system. The term sub-caste is sometimes used. However, the madiga as a whole have criticized the use of the term. A number of castes together constitute the Scheduled Caste category, they claim.

Jambavapuranam

the madiga believe that Jambava came into being before the earth, the sky and the waters existed and that he created the three gods: Brahma, Vishnu and Eshwar. The madiga are his descendents. The Jambavapuranam is a collection of originary myths of the madiga. This collection is not in the form of an 'epic' of the Ramayana or Mahabharata type. It does not have a religious significance either—it is rather about the identity and original importance of the madiga caste. For this reason, the Jambavudu is referred to not as Jambava devudu (god) but as Jambavathatha (grandpa) or Jambavamuni (sage). The madiga cultural identity is marked by allegiance to Jambava as the origin of humanity, i.e., the aadi manavudu (the first man) who emerges from the Jambudweepam (Jambu island). Legend has it that once the Hindu sage Vishwamitra and Jambava, sitting on two hills, entered into a debate and the former defeated Jambava through deceit. Unlike the Ramayana, which separates humanity into different castes and communities in political and social isolation from each other, the Jambavapuranam is about the association of different caste groups. In these myths, each caste is related to Jambavudu through a specific cultural genealogy, and the link is usually through leather. The recent popularization of the Jambavapuranam has increased the rate of accretion of new stories that relate it to contemporary history, and in this trend a Hinduization has also been attempted. However, these initiatives have not succeeded. The dakkali retain the Jambava legend on palm-leaf manuscripts. Recently the Jambavapuranam has been rendered in print by Jayadheer Tirumala Rao.

Jatra
large, often very large, annual gatherings and festivities focused on a local deity

Jeldi
a water-related festival exclusively of the baindla, celebrations for which often included pots

Karnam
keeper of records of land ownership and use; uses a sort of joint handwriting illegible to others; they are brahman

Katta Mysamma
a village deity, guardian of the embankment

Kinnera
the kinnera is a stringed instrument native to the nomadic tribes in the Deccan plateau, such as the dakkali and the chenchu. A kinnera performance involves vocals and music, and the ballads are sung primarily in rustic Telugu

Komati
trading and business caste

Kothalu

a proportion of the newly harvested grain that is customarily taken from the untouchable castes

Koora

a curry, vegetable or meat accompaniment for rotte or rice

Kshatriya

a ruling group/caste

Kunchi, kulla

a kind of head covering made with layers of old cloth. At dawn when women go out to sweep, it protects their heads from the chill; towards the end of the day, it serves as a container to carry back the paddy they have earned.

Madiga

a group of castes, comprising untouchable agricultural labourers, leather workers; in these stories also musicians, dancers, performers. Chindu is a madiga caste. They are the keepers of caste history and bagotam performers. Dakkali is another madiga caste.

Mala

untouchable village servants and agricultural labourers; they are a group of castes.

Mantra-tantra

amulet, with a mantra inside it

Manyam

lands gifted to dalits in recognition of vetti and other services performed for the village, in the pre-independence (Nizam) period; manyam lands are cultivated by rotation.

Metari

a community or jaati elder

Mota bavi

field well; this is a large agricultural or field well. Such wells can be up to half an acre in diameter. The walls of the well are built up with stone (granite) and the steps leading to the water are often a series of long granite slabs protruding out of the walls. Water is drawn using a very large aspherical metal bucket called a bokkena. It has a wide hole at the bottom, to which a large leather pipe called the thondam (elephant's trunk) is connected. The lower end of the leather bucket is knotted on to a thick rope (of eight to ten inches diameter) which automatically closes when the bucket is lowered into the water. When the bucket is raised, the system opens the knot so that the water is let into the irrigation canal. The bucket is raised and lowered by bullocks drawing the rope over a big pulley mounted on a large iron frame that is fixed on a platform that overhangs the water at one side. The platform is usually built with stone, sometimes covered with brick and mortar. This platform is located on the high end of the well's wall (usually built up with excavated earth). It is also located over the deepest point of the well to ensure water is always available to the bokkena. Jumping off the platform or the iron frame is both the safest in terms of depth, and also a mark of the diver's courage since it is from a great height. This mechanism was replaced by the diesel engine pump.

Neeretollu

they are watermen. Traditionally belonging to the mala community, they were required to look after the tank and were given inam land as payment for this work.

Netakaanollu

a mala caste of weavers.

Ooru Jeruvu

village tanks; the relatively dry areas of what are today northern Karnataka and south-western Andhra Pradesh were irrigated through a series of upper-riparian tanks, sometimes linked through canals, that were built during the Vijayanagara period (1346–1550s) and maintained through the period of Kutub Shahi and Asaf Jahi (1550s–1947) rule in these areas that were part of the pre-independence Hyderabad state. These tanks are rain-fed (as against the older lower-riparian tanks in the river deltas) and made possible the opening up of dry and primarily pastoral areas for agriculture. Nineteenth century British surveys document a very large number of these tanks spread over the entire region. Some of them were large enough to irrigate thousands of acres. When maintained properly, these tanks were perennial and enabled the cultivation of cash crops such as cotton and indigo. In the areas that lay below the height of the tank, it was possible even to grow rice. Temples and upper caste families generally held these irrigated lands while the lower castes cultivated rain-fed lands. Tanks were a centre of village life. Without adequate maintenance, many of these tanks dried or silted up in the latter part of the twentieth century (older people in the village remember them in their prime). Irrigation and water resources were key issues that led to the formation of a separate Telangana state. The argument was that when new dams were built in coastal Andhra, not only were Telangana's water resources diverted, its extensive irrigation system was also laid to waste.

Palodu, edurupalodu and avathalodu

(in "But Why Shouldn't the Baindla Woman Ask for Land?") all three groups are madiga. Palodu and edurupalodu refer to people who are closely related: they share work, and participate in family get-togethers and ceremonies. When the vetti system of bonded or unpaid labour prevailed in the Deccan region, it functioned through a system of rotation. Thus in alternate years or alternate seasons, one group would have the responsibility/privilege of cultivating a piece of land, serving at the landlord's homestead, etc. Within the community, the one who holds the vetti at a particular point of time is called palodu and the one who does not is the edurupalodu. Avathalodu is also part of this vetti but the person is not so closely related and thus not part of familial activities. Vetti was abolished after independence in 1947, but continues to be practised in many places.

Pandiri
shelter constructed out of branches and leaves—like a pandal or tent

Panipatalollu
literally 'working–singing people'; refers to sabbanda and mala-madiga together

Pantulu
teachers

Patel
a generic term for an upper caste villager

Patwari
assistant to the dora

Poligoliga, poligalugani
'may the village flourish/May the crops be plentiful!'

Putti (of rice/paddy)
a putti consists of twenty sacks of hundred kilograms each; in some areas it may be a little less; also a sack of paddy could weigh less than a sack of rice.

Ra, Orey, Osey

though these forms of address are acceptable in intimate and affectionate relationships, they are insulting when used in other contexts, and more so when addressing an older person. The suffixes –vaadu, –odu and –adi, which take different inflections in different words—for instance chinduloda, dakkaloda—are also demeaning. Upper castes routinely use these forms to address mala-madiga people. They also demean and show contempt through the use of 'half-names' such as Elli (for Ellamma in "Ellamma is Distressed"), Antiga (for Antappa in "But Why Shouldn't the Baindla Woman Ask for her Land?"), Baliga (for Balappa in "Raw Wound") and so on. Even high-caste children would address a dalit elder by his/her name in diminutive, quite like a white youth would address a black elder as 'boy' during the days of slavery in the United States. However, when used by dalits to address fellow-dalits, the same diminutive would be a sign of affection, as seen in the story "Trace It!" where Pentadu, Chandrudu, Sammadu are used as endearments for Pentaiah, Chandraiah, Samaiah. Similarly a person called Muthyalaiah can be 'Muthyalanna' (anna meaning elder brother) to a fellow-dalit and can even be shortened to 'Muthyalu', as happens in "A Beauteous Light".

Rachchabanda

village square; the place where panchayats are held and where people gather to discuss village affairs

Razakars

Muslim militia in Hyderabad, headed by the powerful Kasim Razvi, before its takeover by the Union of India in 1948. In these stories, told from a dalit point of view, the term 'Razakar' refers more generally to the alliance of landlords, bureaucracy, rulers and militia that held power. This was the alliance under attack in the Telangana armed struggle of the 1940s in which rural dalits were the principal actors. The term is also often used in casual speech to denote the period before Hyderabad became part of the Indian Union.

Reddy, kamma, velama, kapu
dominant farming castes

Rotte
flat bread roasted on a griddle; usually made from a millet (jowari, ragi)

Sabbanda
artisanal castes, also agricultural labourers; not untouchable; sometimes referred to as sudrollu (sudra). Described in administrative schedules as Backward Classes (BCs) or Other Backward Classes (OBC), these include:

Golla: shepherd
Mangali: barber
Chakali: washerperson
Dudekala: a sabbanda caste of Telugu-speaking cotton cleaners who are Muslim
Gaundla, gauda, eediga: toddy-tapper
Balija: a land-owning caste; today often teachers
Besta: fisher people
Kummari: potter
Kammari: blacksmith
Mudiraju, mutrasi: fruit and vegetable sellers
Salé, padmasalé: weavers
Mandahechu and gangireddhulollu: sudra/OBC

Shuddhi karma
purification rites, practised by the brahman after a caste or other defilement

Shuddhi Nilayam

enclosure where a brahman being 'purified' is kept in isolation

Tataki

in the Hindu epic, Ramayana, Tataki is a rakshasi (demon) and Rama kills her on the pretext that she is disrupting the rituals of the sages. But dalits argue that she was a dalit and an original inhabitant of the forestlands which were colonized by the upper castes. Even Valmiki seems to have mentioned that she had the power of one thousand elephants and took care of the forests. Since she fought against the upper caste occupation of the forestlands and their plunder, she was branded a rakshasi.

Thatha

grandfather; often also used to address a respected elder

Thunga

there are two types of thunga-grass: one that grows in the tanks and streams, which is a thick, tall variety and is not eaten by cattle; and the other that grows in fields, which is soft, which cattle do eat. Both types are referred to in the stories.

Vetti

forced labour—in pre-independence Telangana, the panipatala castes were forced to give such regular and free labour. In 'return' they were allowed to cultivate small inam or manyam lands, to be rotated among themselves.

Wada, keri, gudem

area outside the village (ooru) in which madiga, mala and other untouchables live; while the term 'wada' has been standardized through the new dalit literature, in regions bordering Karnataka the term 'keri' is used. 'Gudem' is used in the areas bordering coastal Andhra and in general for tribal settlements.

Yama

god of death

A NOTE ON THE TRANSLATION

These stories are written in a variant of Telugu used by dalits in the Tandur region of western Telangana. Academic and official Telugu is sanskritized and has an upper caste, Andhra slant. The placing of the Tandur variant on the written page involves considerable artistry and not a little technical effort since it involves open battles and subtler skirmishes with the history of the standardization of official Telugu, its grammar, vocabulary, orthography, and even punctuation. Shyamala speaks constantly of her delight in 'remembering' a word, a phrase, a tone, a linguistic pun or joke.

The historical hub that enables this linguistic intervention is the coming together of (i) the Madiga Dandora in the mid-1990s with the demand for categorization of the Scheduled Castes for more equitable access to reservation in education and employment; (ii) the movement for a separate state (which concluded with the formation of Telangana in 2014) in which the cultural domination of Telangana by Andhra was a key issue; (iii) the growth of the dalit movement in the 1990s, and of course, earlier (iv) feminist and (v) naxalite movements in these areas.

Each of these contributes to, and is in turn serviced by, the aesthetic of these stories, and the author's journey of self-discovery is also the refurbishing of a world and a community for this new moment. Educated readers of Telugu are baffled and exasperated by the strangeness of Shyamala's language even as they are charmed by its freshness, its vitality, and the laughs that appear where no one thought there would be one. The author's enjoyment—in the rehabilitation of her mother tongue, her caste, and her world as a lived place—is only too evident. It may not be so obvious that this return involves critical engagement with reformist, gandhian, administrative–developmental, and even ambedkarian representations of the village—in brief with the history of the twentieth century.

Creating (or finding) a variant of English[3] that would not just mimic the strangeness that an educated reader of Telugu experiences, but actually carry the multiplicitous charge of the original, was a challenge that translation is not yet ready for. That is a loss. However, these translations have tried to maintain an alertness to the cultural politics of these stories. By translating the stories into a form of standard English, the translators have looked past the educated Telugu reader's estrangement, endorsed the author's pleasure in the reclamation of her tongue, and accorded the Tandur variant the status and dignity of a full-fledged language. That is a gain.

---

3. All caste/jaati terms have been lower-cased in these stories; italics have not been used for Telugu words. For Telugu words that appear in the plural, an 's' is not added—this would amount to treating a Telugu word as an English word. So madiga could be both singular and plural depending on context, unless on occasion the Telugu plural is used, such as chindollu for chindu.

LINES THAT CUT TO THE VERY GUT

K. Lalita

Gogu Shyamala's stories are a treasure-house of knowledge, skills, music and aesthetics of dalit life that are invisible to the rest of society. Stories such as these can come only from a life lived in a dalit world. They provide a window for us to peep in, to grasp, to understand, to digest and sort out. They leave us in awe, amazement, happiness and pain—all at once. The images and imagery come from the author's lived experiences that are in tension with the 'universal', with rich descriptions of skills that range from producing everyday needs to effortless ways of forgetting hunger. These stories do not have an explicit political purpose; they weave lives and small pleasures together with everyday work, life, relationships, food, play, music and culture. Here the individual has an organic connection with her family and community.

Shyamala's way of telling a story is refreshingly different. Dealing with children growing up in often hostile worlds, her stories are like the tiny, beautiful, multi-coloured wild flowers she reminisces about from her childhood. They have the freshness and fragrance of the wet earth after the first showers. They are earthy, sensual. They redefine body and beauty; sadness and happiness; work and leisure; merit and pride. Her stories are crafted such that they do not fit within any proclaimed ideological frame. The narratives point to new directions that signify the political without being pedagogic.

Her first story "Enuganta Tandri Kanna Ekula Buttanta Talli Nayam" (translated in this volume as *Father May Be an Elephant and Mother Only a Small Basket, But...*), published in 2002 in *Bhumika*, a monthly journal, was much appreciated by her readers for its feminist sensibility. The story—revolving around her mother, father and grandmother—helps Shyamala give full play to her experiences as a child: it opens with an idyll and ends in a scene of domestic violence. Shyamala was later amused when she saw a critic's comment that the conclusion highlighted a dalit woman's oppression. She felt it was completely unintentional and she did not mean to show her father in poor light.

Often, classics in short story writing, from both Indian and world literature, are products of the authors' cerebral worlds. Even when there is an attempt to recreate the physical and emotional worlds of the marginalized sections, they often remain interpretations. The themes in Shyamala's stories are varied, drawn from the worlds dalit communities inhabit, imbued with the flesh and blood of dalit lives and culture. Shyamala's stories seem to inaugurate a new genre of "little stories" that speak of, in feminist scholar Susie Tharu's words, the "world of the little, subaltern traditions, as against that of the great traditions".

These stories—filled with nuanced descriptions of livestock and wild animals, crops, food, rituals—completely change our understanding of rural ecology and environment. We have one story where the village tank is the narrator, and she laments: "They dig bore-wells, cutting into my womb." Shyamala's stories challenge notions that mainstream society holds dear. Ideas like 'merit', 'hard work' and 'self-respect' are turned upside down. The children, men and women Shyamala brings alive in her fiction are strong and persevering, yet vulnerable.

The stories propose a way of life that has a great deal of humour while forcing open the worlds we never see otherwise —the world of dalit customs, everyday life, traditions and rituals. We also see in a story like "Trace It!" ("Jaada" in Telugu), how music is an intrinsic part of dalit life; how 'song and work' (*pani-paata*) coexist for the labouring castes. Shyamala believes that the language she had known as a child, though some part of it has disappeared now, is the only way to recreate the worlds her memories inhabit. This is the language her elders spoke. This is the language that reflects a way of life—a life of work centred on agriculture, livestock, and lakes; a life where hunger lurks in every corner. Shyamala's Telugu showcases some of the terms, concepts and words that were once in use; a language that might be facing extinction. This recalls Marathi dalit writer Arun Kamble's anguish in the poem "Which Language should I Speak",[4] where the grandfather hollers:

> 'You whore-son, talk like we do!
> Talk, I tell you!'
> Picking through the Vedas
> his top-knot well-oiled with ghee
> my Brahmin teacher tells me
> 'You idiot, use the language correctly!'
> Now I ask you,
> Which language should I speak?

For Shyamala, her stories are not just about memories of her childhood—she needs to visualize that world, and grab it from the deep recesses of her mind. Phrases she uses such as *deemana goyyalole urkutundru* (in "Father May Be...") referring

---

4. Translated by Priya Adarkar. See *Poisoned Bread: Translations from Modern Marathi Literature*, Ed. Arjun Dangle (Orient Longman, Hyderabad: 1992), 54.

to children darting around like dragonflies that signify speed and alertness; *sabbanda kulalu*, (in "Jambava's Lineage") referring to the productive castes (such as dalit and Other Backward Classes); *takanadaalante* (in "Madiga Badeyya") to collide with or confront the upper castes—are expressions even readers of standard Telugu would not be familiar with. The narrative, its idiom, theme and characters are rendered in a special language. As explained in the note on the translation, she uses a variant of Telugu used by dalits in the Tandur region of western Telangana. For instance, *paska tokkocchindi* is an expression used for walking on wild grass as opposed to walking on well laid out roads in the city. Similar expressions open up a whole world of difference between rural and urban life; they gently point to the privileges urban folk take for granted, compared to the life of the rural poor. This is the idiom she chronicles as a writer, capturing along with it a world that seems to be fading away—the tanks, the commons, the crops, flowers, fruits, plants, vegetables, greens, work implements, and the songs and games children played. What is notable is she does this without nostalgia—for the rural world of western Telangana, like perhaps any other part of India, is brutal to dalits. Shyamala says she has been able to capture this idiom only with her dalit and feminist consciousness and not because of her earlier involvement with Left class politics.

While Shyamala's stories are not overtly didactic, we are coaxed into learning lessons from them. Work is not a painful thing, but a life-defining activity. Drought leads to worry and depression. Rains are important for mental health (not just for agriculture). Everyone has an important and special place in the family. Affection for children and getting them involved in productive labour are two sides of the same coin. In the universe Shyamala recreates, children are never given stale food.

Think of endless discussions about government programmes for food security failing to provide a normal, decent, cooked meal to children in government schools!

Despite the fact that Gogu Shyamala has been writing for less than a decade her contributions have been significant. In 2003, she edited an anthology of dalit women's writings called *Nallappoddu: Dalitha Sthreela Sahithyam 1921–2002* (Black Dawn: Dalit Women's Writings, 1921–2002). This was followed by *Nallaregatisallu: Madiga MadigaUpakulala Aadolla Kathalu* (Furrows in Black Soil: The Stories of Madiga and Madiga Subcaste Women) in 2006. Two of her stories —"Braveheart Badeyya", "Tataki Wins Again"—appeared in *Different Tales* (2008), an Anveshi project that featured stories from the lives of children who rarely find place in mainstream children's literature. In 2011, she published a biography of one of Telangana's leading dalit politicians, T.N. Sadalakshmi (*Nene Balaanni, T.N. Sadalakshmi Bathuku Katha*), based on a series of interviews with her.

Born in 1969 in Peddamul in Rangareddy district, of erstwhile Andhra Pradesh, Shyamala's childhood appears to be like that of any other dalit girl's, save for her family's decision to send her to a school away from her village. Her family realized that she did not have the physical strength to work in the fields. In Shyamala's words, "I was a weak child—having no strength required for hard labour and I couldn't work like other children." Her brother was a bonded labourer with a rich farmer's family, and her father was a daily-wage labourer. Her mother worked as an agricultural labourer and took care of home as well. Shyamala says they wanted to educate her so that she would have a restful life. She was admitted in a social welfare residential school.

Shyamala studied till intermediate (Class 12) and discontinued as she was drawn to various democratic movements such as the Marxist-Leninist movement, the women's movement and the dalit movement, with specific involvement in the Madiga Dandora movement (which demanded the subdivision of the benefits of reservation within Scheduled Caste communities in Andhra Pradesh). She returned to her studies much later, acquiring a law degree in 2006. Currently the coordinator of the dalit initiative at the Anveshi Research Centre for Women's Studies in Hyderabad, Shyamala continues to make significant contributions as an activist and as a writer. Her political presence in all these struggles has contributed in raising newer challenges and questions for identity politics.

THE TRANSLATORS

Diia Rajan lives in Hyderabad and works on issues of gender and development. This is her first attempt at translation, inspired by the intricate beauty of Shyamala's craft, the music of her language, and the rhythm and humour of her stories. ("Father May Be an Elephant and Mother Only a Small Basket, But..." and "Trace It!")

Sashi Kumar has been working with NGOs for over 20 years, prior to which he worked in banking for a decade. He says, 'I find Shyamala's work striking because her stories have universal themes set in contexts and around events that cannot be imagined unless one has lived in them—so they have both a ring of familiarity and an exoticism that is very attractive.' ("But Why Shouldn't the Baindla Woman Ask for Her Land")

A. Suneetha is a senior fellow at the Anveshi Research Centre for Women's Studies, Hyderabad. She is drawn to Shyamala's stories due to several reasons—'the richness of her description of dalit life-world; understated philosophical reflections that one comes across at unexpected junctures in the stories; her serious but delightful take on children's ways; quiet humour, and of course, her wonderful Telugu (there are so many new words that I learnt while translating).' ("Braveheart Badeyya" and "A Beauteous Light")

N. Manohar Reddy has worked as lecturer in English in India and Saudi Arabia and has also been guest faculty at the University of Hyderabad. After a Ph.D. in Cultural Studies at the English and Foreign Languages University, Hyderabad, he now teaches at the Nalsar University of Law in Hyderabad. 'I see Shyamala's use of language as part of a larger attempt by the dalit literary tradition to reconstitute Telugu language as a site of egalitarian politics.' ("Jambava's Lineage")

R. Srivatsan is a senior fellow at the Anveshi Research Centre for Women's Studies. He translates selectively for projects and friends he has a special commitment to. His close association with Shyamala and her intellectual trajectory provides the background for his translations of her work. 'These translations have in each case resulted in a deepening of my own understanding of caste, culture and hegemony in contemporary India.' ("Tataki Wins Again" and "Raw Wound")

Gita Ramaswamy works with the Hyderabad Book Trust in publishing alternative, low-cost literature in Telugu. She is the author of *India Stinking* (2004) and has co-authored *Taking Charge of Our Bodies* (2001) and *On Their Own* (2003). What drew her to Shyamala's stories was 'the little girl in the story—the ability to go back in time and see the child in oneself.' ("The Village Tank's Lament")

Uma Bhrugubanda teaches in the Department of Cultural Studies at the English and Foreign Languages University, Hyderabad. Reading Shyamala's stories for the first time she was struck by the absolutely new world that her stories opened up. 'Here were men, women and children too, battling against an oppressive world with uncommon courage and resourcefulness supported only by the love and affection of their family and community. Shyamala displays an intimate and vivid knowledge of the lives of Telangana dalits and their relation to the land, to different professions and to education. From Shyamala's perspective, dalits no longer remain victims; rather the ingenuity, skill and art that structures their daily lives are revealed to us in rich detail. Translating her work has been a pleasure, a challenge, and above all a learning experience.' ("Obstacle Race")

P. Pavana has been active in the women's movement and has, for many years, been a part of the editorial collective of *Mahila Margam*, a Telugu magazine with a wide circulation. She teaches English in a private college in Hyderabad. She says, 'I belong to the Telangana region and have a good grasp of the Telugu spoken there. I consider Shyamala to be one of the most significant new short story writers in Telugu.' ("Ellamma is Distressed")

Duggirala Vasanta is professor of linguistics at Osmania University. She has been translating for several years and takes on projects that she is interested in or committed to. 'The discussions on translation of some of the stories included in the Different Tales project of Anveshi, on which I worked, provided the larger context for me to translate Shyamala's story in this volume.' ("The Bottom of the Well")

ACKNOWLEDGEMENTS

"If you get your children educated, who will slog for free in our fields?" Under such pressure from the karnam, reddy and other dora of the village, my eldest brother Ramacendrappa was forced into agricultural labour. One day, on his way back from the fields, he was struck by lightning and died. And my younger brother Laxman was forced to take his place. Slogging their backs off, staving off hunger, with no support to lean on, my mother Ananthamma and father Balappa ensured that I got a higher education. My grandmother Sangamma laboured all day for the right to scour leftover broken grains from sand and ensure some food in our bellies. My sister Anasuja sheltered our home like an elder son. I am indebted to all of them.

I owe thanks to well-wishers and relatives in my village— the Backward Classes and peasants, the poor people of the dominant castes and of my birth keri— who figure as characters in my stories. I thank Prof Susie Tharu for respecting and admiring my stories and for giving shape to this volume and making it see the light of day. I thank K. Lalita who has written an insightful Afterword. Special thanks to each of the translators—Diia Rajan, Sashi Kumar, A. Suneetha, N. Manohar Reddy, R. Srivatsan, Gita Ramaswamy, Uma Bhrugabanda, P. Pavana and Duggirala Vasanta—who generously and enthusiastically agreed to translate my 'difficult' language and encouraged me with their support. Also to K.

Balagopal who had agreed to translate a story; but his sudden death deprived us of the honour of carrying that translation.

I am grateful to friends who have been teaching some of these stories in their university courses—Deepa Patnaik and Manohar Reddy of Central University, Hyderabad, and Raju Naik and K. Satyanarayana of the English and Foreign Languages University, Hyderabad. I thank the Anveshi Research Centre for Women for help and support on various occasions.

The following journals encouraged me by publishing my stories—*Bhumika*, *Sahitya Prasthanam*, *Pratighatana*, *Mana Telangana* and *Nigha*. Also, the online magazine, *Pranahita*. I owe them thanks.

For support and critical discussions, thanks to Swathy Margaret, Jalli Indira, Nagamma Phule, Veena Shatrugna, Rama Melkote, K. Sajaya, Panusuri Ravinder, A. Vidyasagar. K. MadhavaRao, Panthakala Srinivas, Vemula Yellaiah, Jilakara Srinivas, Batukutadu Srinivas, Gurram Sitaram, T. Devaki Devi, K. Vimala, Jagan Reddy, Nandini Sidareddy, B.S. Ramulu, Katti Padmarao, Abburi Chayadevi, Mudiganti Sujata Reddy, Volga, Alladi Uma and Sridhar, Suneetha Rani, Gorusu Jagadeeshwar Reddy, Ammangi Venugopal, Ainala Saidulu Amrutalatha, Alivelu Manga, Domala Mallesh, Dappolla Ramesh and Venkanna Sabbanda.

I wish to thank the Asmita Resource Centre for Women who selected my story "Radam" (featured in this collection as "Raw Wound") as one of the best stories to be written in Andhra Pradesh.

I acknowledge the support of my in-laws, my sisters-in-law, my children Ravikant and Roshanaditya, and my partner Vijay Kumar—all of whom set aside the demands they had of me when I was in the process of writing these stories.

Finally, thanks to Navayana for producing this volume with care, love and beauty.

GOGU SHYAMALA
13 December 2011

ISBN (paperback) 9781911284741

ISBN (ebook) 9781911284734

A catalogue record for this book is available from the British Library.

Cover art by Malvika Raj

Cover design by Aude Nasr

Edited by S. Anand

Typesetting and ebook production by Abbas Jaffary

Made with Hederis

Printed and bound by Severnprint Ltd

ABOUT TILTED AXIS PRESS

Tilted Axis is a non-profit press publishing mainly work by Asian writers, translated into a variety of Englishes. This is an artistic project, for the benefit of readers who would not otherwise have access to the work – including ourselves. We publish what we find personally compelling.

Founded in 2015, we are based in the UK, a state whose former and current imperialism severely impacts writers in the majority world. This position, and those of our individual members, informs our practice, which is also an ongoing exploration into alternatives – to the hierarchisation of certain languages and forms, including forms of translation; to the monoculture of globalisation; to cultural, narrative, and visual stereotypes; to the commercialisation and celebrification of literature and literary translation.

We value the work of translation and translators through fair, transparent pay, public acknowledgement, and respectful communication. We are dedicated to improving access to the industry, through translator mentorships, paid publishing internships, open calls and guest curation.

Our publishing is a work in progress – we are always open to feedback, including constructive criticism, and suggestions for collaborations. We are particularly keen to connect with Black and indigenous translators of Asian languages.

tiltedaxispress.com
@TiltedAxisPress